She glared up at him.

'Three hours in town and already she's reforming rural medicine,' Steve said with hateful cynicism.

A slow, burning anger began to take hold of Jo. 'All three of those people will be out of hospital faster if they can be kept together as a family unit.'

'You don't take over until the day after tomorrow and up till then, whether you like it or not, what I say goes,' was the prompt reply.

Dear Reader

This month we touch upon personal grief for the heroines in TROUBLED HEARTS by Christine Adams, and SUNLIGHT AND SHADOW by Frances Crowne, both handled with sensitivity. PARTNERS IN PRIDE by Drusilla Douglas and A TESTING TIME (set in Australia) by Meredith Webber give us heroines who are trying hard to make a fresh start in life, not always an easy thing to do—we think you'll both laugh and cry.

The Editor

Having pursued many careers—from schoolteaching to pig farming—with varying degrees of success and plenty of enjoyment, **Meredith Webber** seized on the arrival of a computer in her house as an excuse to turn to what had always been a secret urge—writing. As she had more doctors and nurses in the family than any other professional people, the medical romance seemed the way to go! Meredith lives on the Gold Coast of Queensland, with her husband and teenage son.

Recent titles by the same author:

HEALING LOVE

A TESTING TIME

BY
MEREDITH WEBBER

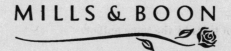

MILLS & BOON LIMITED
ETON HOUSE, 18–24 PARADISE ROAD
RICHMOND, SURREY, TW9 1SR

First published in Great Britain 1994
by Mills & Boon Limited

© Meredith Webber 1994

Australian copyright 1994   Philippine copyright 1994
This edition 1994

ISBN 0 263 78605 6

Set in 10 on 11½ pt Linotron Times
03-9406-55853

Typeset in Great Britain by Centracet, Cambridge
Made and printed in Great Britain

CHAPTER ONE

JO HEARD the wailing of the sirens first, coming eerily closer in the muted light of dusk. They echoed in her ears like the cries of a wounded animal, lost in this lonely wasteland that was 'the bush'. When flashing red and blue lights filled her rear-view mirror, she pulled carefully off the narrow strip of bitumen that formed a road out here in the far west of Queensland. Screaming their urgency, a police car and a dull yellow ambulance streaked past.

More customers, she thought ruefully, shuddering at the thought of what the ambulance might contain. With deft precision she swung the heavily laden car back off the rough gravel verge and followed, her leisurely journey towards Warilla now a concentrated dash. Although the doctor covering the hospital would have been alerted when the ambulance left town, an ambulance invariably meant an emergency, and emergencies meant all available help should be on hand.

She drove as fast as she dared, pleased to have her mind diverted from the depressing thoughts that had haunted her long journey. Even speeding, she was falling behind the emergency vehicles and their tail-lights soon disappeared from view. She was alone once more.

Suddenly, in the swiftly darkening gloom, a tall water tower rose like a sentinel above the flat plain. In the same way that a lighthouse welcomed sailors back to land, these water towers marked the scattered pockets of civilisation in the unending miles of seemingly empty land.

5

Street-lights were on as she entered Warilla, and turned left at a sign into the hospital grounds. She reached into the back seat and separated a bright blue and white checked gown from the pile of clothes lying across her carefully stacked luggage. Clutching this unconventional garment, she climbed stiffly out of the driver's seat and stretched herself before crossing the short distance to the brightly lit doorway.

'I'm Jo Armitage, the new doctor,' she told the young sister who eyed her enquiringly as she walked into the wide foyer, still decorated with Christmas tinsel on this third day after New Year. 'The ambulance passed me as I drove into town. Can you use an extra hand?'

'Can we? I'm Karen Short. Dr Hemming is here, but it was a head-on with a family of three in one car and a young lad in the other. The police car brought in two of them! Steve — that's Dr Hemming — is working on the young fellow, but I don't think there's much hope.' She shook her head, then shrugged her shoulders, putting aside personal thoughts to concentrate on professionalism.

'We've got the family comfortable, but both parents are in pain — breaks most likely — and their daughter's unconscious. You can wash in here — the X-rays should be through by now; I'll get them for you.'

As she spoke she led the way to a small ante-room, and waved her hand towards the wash-basin fixed to one wall. Her initial relief at finding extra help on hand was now waning and Jo felt, rather than saw, that a wary inventory was being taken.

'Are you certain you want to start right now?' Karen asked, and Jo turned to grin at her.

'Wondering if a five-foot-four female in a skimpy

hot-pink playsuit could really be the new hospital superintendent?'

'No! No, of course not!' the flustered girl replied hastily.

'It's a long, hot drive and this is the most comfortable garment I own,' Jo explained. 'I really am the Dr Armitage you're expecting to start work on Monday, and, yes, I'm quite certain I'm ready to start now. Whether I want to or not is probably immaterial.'

Three hours later she wondered at the stamina of the human body. She had driven for nearly twelve hours to finish her journey rather than spend a second night on the road, yet had managed to find the extra energy to do what was required of her with a professional expertise.

Mr and Mrs Andrews were resting as comfortably as their plasters would allow, and her main concern now was with their young daughter, who remained unconscious.

'Is Dr Hemming still in Theatre?' she asked Karen, who came in as she stood watching the child.

The sister nodded, her eyes on the still, slight form under the sheet.

'I'd better scrub up and go in — maybe there's something I can do to help.'

She hoped the nurse could not hear the reluctance in her voice. To face a possibly dying young man on the operating table was the last thing her exhausted body felt like!

'I'm sure Steve would appreciate it,' Karen responded with a cheerful grin. 'I'll stay with Jenny.'

Jo sighed and nodded.

'None of the tests I've done shows skull or brain stem damage, but she needs half-hourly obs. Call me at once if her pupils react at all sluggishly to light — it could be the first sign of a build-up of pressure within the cranium.'

'Let's hope not!' Karen replied, unable, like all caring professionals, to escape the extra tug of sympathy towards children who were sick or injured. 'Matron came on when the call came for the ambulance. She's in Theatre with Steve. You'll find a cap, gown and mask in the little ante-room between the plaster-room where we were and the theatre. Will you want help to scrub up?'

'I'll put on sterile gear and go in first. They may not need me!'

'Some hope!' was the wry response, and Jo felt a warm complicity. A strange feeling of belonging stirred her tired body and regenerated her flagging energy.

Theatre garb came in one size in Warilla—extra large! Enveloped in a neck-to-ankle gown, with an outsize cap pulled over her short brown hair, and a mask covering all of her face except a pair of cheeky brown eyes, she pushed open the door of the theatre and knew immediately that she was too late.

A battle had been fought and lost in that small room this night, and the heavy despair of defeat hovered like a cloud over the two people who moved with tired automation, packing away instruments and equipment while a wardsman wheeled the body of the young man out of a side-door.

'I'm sorry, Rosie, but I'll have to leave the rest of this to you. There were three other people in that accident. I've wasted enough time already tonight.'

There was a harsh bitterness in the deep voice, and a depth of anger that puzzled Jo. She pulled off her mask and spoke swiftly.

'The others are all OK,' she said, not bothering with any polite preliminaries when she could ease his concern. 'I'm Jo Armitage. I followed the ambulance into town and arrived in time to handle both the adults. Mrs Andrews has a simple fracture of the radius and ulna in her left arm—she must have been turning around to the little girl in the back seat when it happened. One ankle is swollen, but there are no broken bones showing on X-ray, so it's been packed in ice and she's actually asleep. Her husband escaped with a broken leg, clean breaks in both tibia and fibula, and he's in plaster.'

The man's eyes snapped up to lock on hers.

Was there a special mystique in eye contact when all other features were hidden from view? Jo wondered. She'd heard theatre nurses discuss the unique thrill of eyes meeting eyes and the secret communion they could achieve within a busy theatre, but she had dismissed such words as nonsense.

With these strange thoughts flickering through her mind, she hesitated, looking up at the tall, bulky figure in the blood-spattered gown who was standing, still as a wax model, staring at her with an unnerving intensity. His mask was still in place, so all she could see was a pair of deep-set eyes, their blue gleam half hidden under heavy lids and veiled by thick, dark lashes.

A small shiver of apprehension trickled up her spine as those eyes finished a cursory survey of her enveloped figure and rose to meet hers again in a clash that jarred her slender form. It was as if some precognition existed between them. Two friends recognising some bond from the past, or two foes saluting before battle?

He reached up to untie his mask, and she watched his hand move, anxious to see his face, yet unable to explain the anxiety. His nose was thickly carved and straight, leading the eye down to a mouth that was compressed into a firm straight line—the mouth of a man holding back some strong emotion.

I must be far more tired than I realised, she thought crossly, banishing these fancies that were foreign to her pragmatic nature.

Hurrying into further explanations to cover her consternation, she rattled on, 'Mr Andrews has been worrying more about his car than his wife and daughter. It's a heavy four-wheel drive, which explains why their injuries aren't more severe. According to him the other car came straight into them, but slid underneath their chassis. He's complaining of pain in the chest region, but an ECG showed nothing so I think it's possibly bruising from his seatbelt. They're both being checked half-hourly for signs of internal bleeding or delayed concussion.'

'And the child?' he barked.

Time for introductions later! Jo thought wryly, anxious to create a good impression but still battling with her errant fancies.

'She's unconscious, but there are no lacerations or signs of fracture, and her reflexes are good. Sister is watching her.'

'You should send her straight down to Yaroona. The flying surgeons are based there, and they have the facilities to do a scan.'

She knew then, without a doubt, that this man could, and would, dominate her if given half a chance, but she was not prepared to let that happen again—not ever! Tilting her chin in an unconscious gesture of defiance, she prepared to fight—politely, of course!

'You didn't send her on when she first came in,' she argued. 'You must have checked them all and started treatment for shock before taking the young man to Theatre.'

Hitting back at him was an instinctive attempt at self-preservation.

'She's been unconscious for another three hours since I saw her. Don't you think more tests might prove beneficial?' He spoke with a crisp edge of sarcasm that scraped along Jo's stretched nerves, leaving her feeling raw and exposed.

'No, I don't!' she responded firmly, pulling her cap off her head and running her fingers through her flattened hair. 'At this stage she needs observation and rest. She can get both here. She also needs to be in the same hospital as her parents, and it was only by promising her mother that we would keep her here unless an emergency occurred that I could persuade her to try to sleep. Don't you think they've had enough trauma without adding mental anguish by splitting them up into different hospitals unnecessarily?'

'Three hours in town and already she's reforming rural medicine,' he said to the air above her head with hateful cynicism.

A slow, burning anger began to take hold of her, but Jo held it in control, determined to fight this arrogant man, and win!

'I may not have your experience of rural medicine, but I have studied patient recovery-rates quite extensively and all three of those people will be out of hospital faster if they can be kept together as a family unit.'

She glared up at him as she snapped the words out, tiredness exacerbating the ridiculous altercation.

'You don't take over until the day after tomorrow and up till then, whether you like it or not, I'm in charge, and what I say goes,' was the prompt reply and Jo gasped, unable to believe that this man was baiting her like this in the middle of the night, in the middle of nowhere, after a hectic evening spent patching up accident victims!

They were still standing in the theatre, although the nurse who had been assisting had beaten a strategic retreat. Looking up at her antagonist, Jo realised why the hospital gowns were all extra large! From her vantage point he was like a small mountain. Could she pit herself against a man like this and hope to win? Would he send the child away to prove his point? She remained silent.

As if accepting some victory, he turned away, removing his cap and revealing thick, dark blond hair, streaked by the sun, so that it resembled a tawny mane and gave him a look of the outdoors that was incongruous among the shining sterility of the operating theatre.

'There are only two nursing staff on duty, and, in a twenty-bed hospital, three extra patients make a big difference. Yet you expect one of those staff members virtually to "special" the child so that she can stay here.' He threw the words over his shoulder, not even bothering to look at her as he said them.

Jo sighed, but knew he had provided an answer.

'I'd be happy to sit up with her,' she said quickly. 'I doubt if I'd sleep much anyway, not knowing if there were any changes. At the first sign of complications, I can call you or send her on to Yaroona, whichever you advise.'

There was a tense silence, stretching between them like a yawning chasm.

'If it's just inter-cranial pressure, we could probably relieve it here, so call me first,' he said abruptly, and walked away from her, leaving her staring at the slowly closing door.

'So much for professional co-operation!' she muttered under her breath, pulling off the gown that straggled round her ankles and hurling it into the bin in one corner of the theatre.

She took a deep steadying breath. This posting to Warilla was important to her. It was an opportunity to experience rural medicine at its most basic, and discover if it really was the field in which she wanted to specialise — always supposing you could call becoming a jack of all trades specialising! If succeeding at Warilla meant putting up with a bad-tempered, overbearing, antagonistic GP, then so be it. No one had ever said all doctors were nice people!

Perhaps it's just as well he left when he did, she thought, grinning at the picture she must present with slim bare brown legs protruding from the abbreviated hemline of her playsuit! On the way back to the ward, she retrieved her coat. It wasn't much longer, but at least its tailored styling lent her an aura of professionalism. She needed a shower to wash off the grime of the journey, and clean clothes to make her feel fresher, but, as sure as she disappeared for even ten minutes, Dr High and Mighty Hemming would reappear and have further cause for complaint!

'I'll sit with her now,' she whispered to Karen. 'You have enough to do without this!'

'Mostly paperwork!' The nurse groaned as she stood up and passed Jo the chart. 'I'll bring you in some supper. Tea or coffee?'

'Coffee, thanks, and a sandwich would save my life.'

Was it the mention of food that did the trick? As she spoke they both became aware of a stirring from the bed, and a small voice saying, 'I'm hungry, too!'

Jo moved to the bedside and bent over the little girl. Her pupils were still slightly dilated, but there was no unevenness in their size. She was looking around and obviously registering the foreign surroundings for her lips began to tremble and her small face puckered as tears welled up in her eyes.

'You're all right, pet,' Jo assured her, 'and so are your mum and dad. There was a little accident in the car and you must have bumped your head, which is why you're in this very special hospital.'

'Why is it a very special hospital?' she asked, her tears diverted by Jo's phrasing.

'Because you're here, of course,' Jo told her with a triumphant grin. She was rewarded with an answering smile, and felt a relaxation in Jenny's grip on her hand.

'Can I see Mum and Dad?'

'Not just yet. It's actually the middle of the night, and they are fast asleep. Your mum hurt her arm and your dad hurt his leg, so you're the only one in the family who hasn't any plaster.'

With gentle insistence Jo established that Jenny remembered not only who she was, but details of their journey prior to the accident. Certain that further complications were unlikely, she sat on with her, telling her stories until she fell into a deep but natural sleep.

Coming quietly out of the room, she met the woman who had been assisting in the theatre, bearing a tray with coffee and sandwiches.

'I'm Rosie Strachan, the matron, Dr Armitage. I'm sorry I haven't been in sooner, but——'

Jo reached out to take the tray, and set it down on a table in the hallway.

'You've had a rough night,' she said with quiet sympathy, seeing the deep lines of strain on the woman's face and the damp smudges where tears had been hastily brushed away. 'Please call me Jo,' she continued, covering the other woman's emotional battle with her own conversation. 'My father's a doctor and Dr Armitage always makes me think people are talking to him.'

She was rewarded with a wan smile.

'The young girl has recovered consciousness and spoken quite lucidly,' she explained. 'She's sleeping now, so I thought I'd find the supper that Karen promised.'

'This is it. I'm sorry we took so long. We're all upset,' Rosie murmured, shaking her head as if to clear it of a thought too hard to comprehend. 'The young lad who was killed is a local. It's such a small town, everyone knows everyone else — his mother went to school with me.'

She paused for a moment, rubbing her hands across her face again as if furious with the tears that filled her eyes, then added vehemently, 'I hate it! I hate this part of the job. I know we can't save everyone, but a young kid like that. . .'

Again she hesitated, and Jo watched in silence, knowing that it was best for Rosie to speak, to verbalise the feelings that were tearing her apart. The matron was a tall woman in her mid-forties, with clear tanned skin and soft brown eyes, reddened by recent weeping, but still full of a quiet confidence. Jo knew instinctively that this type of outburst would be rare, and recognised that she was in the right place at the right time. A woman like Rosie Strachan would be more likely to display her feelings to a stranger like herself than to her other colleagues.

'I feel so angry!' Rosie burst out, breaking the silence that had lengthened between them. 'Angry with Lance for killing himself like that! For bringing such agony on his parents! That's stupid, isn't it? To be angry with someone who's just died?'

'I think it's probably very healthy,' Jo assured her.

'I'll do a quick check on the child then come back to have this coffee. Perhaps there's somewhere we could sit together. A hot cup of tea or coffee might help you relax after all you've been doing.'

Rosie nodded, waving a hand towards a door at the end of the hallway. 'The kitchen's through there. It's our home away from home on night duty.'

'You go ahead and I'll join you in a few minutes.'

Reassured that Jenny was sleeping normally, Jo made her way towards the big country-style kitchen, hoping that the questions she wanted to ask Matron about the town and the hospital would successfully divert her mind from the horror of the young man's death.

It was an hour before she returned to the ward to take up her vigil. Rosie Strachan was assuring herself that all was well, before leaving for her home and what remained of a night's sleep. All three of the newcomers were resting peacefully. Slumped in the chair beside Jenny's bed, Jo reviewed the information Rosie had given her.

Warilla sounded like a strongly bound community, providing the rural population of the surrounding area with the facilities of 'town'. Here the graziers' wives shopped, their children went to school, they visited the dentist and arranged with their agent for sale of wool or stock. Like most western towns, it existed because of the rich pastoral country surrounding it, and the country people found their lives a little easier because the town was there.

Now a new phenomenon had given Warilla a boost. Suddenly, the outback had become a tourist attraction and more and more people were travelling west, anxious to see how generations of Australians had lived since the days of early settlement. They came on camping tours, or dropped off the long-distance coaches heading north and west to Darwin, to spend a few days in the town, or visiting local grazing properties. Tourists had discovered Warilla, and, according to Matron Strachan, had brought a much needed prosperity to the small community.

The one subject that wasn't discussed was Dr Steve Hemming, for, although Jo longed to know more about the man who would be her closest professional contact in this isolated town, she could not bring herself to indulge in anything that might be classed as gossip. Her own recent experience had left wounds that gossip had ripped open and memories that gossip had poisoned, leaving her so devastated that the offer of a relieving position at Warilla had seemed like the answer to a prayer.

Jo could see the sky lightening through the window above Jenny's bed and hear the increase in the activity outside that heralded the end of a long night for those on duty. Rising stiffly, she walked out into the hallway, where Karen greeted her.

'There's no change in either of your other patients,' she said quietly. 'Why don't you go home?'

'That's the best suggestion I have ever heard,' Jo told her. 'I'm sure I would if only I knew where "home" was.'

'Oh, you poor thing! You haven't even seen the house! Wait right here while I tell the nurse where I'm going and I'll take you over and show you around.'

Jo propped herself against the wall as waves of tiredness washed over her.

'It's just at the back of the hospital,' Karen explained, leading the way through the kitchen and out into the dusty back yard. 'Steve lived here when he first came to town, but when he resigned he bought a house that he's converted into a surgery and a flat. He lives there when he's in town.'

Just as well, Jo thought, her memories of the clash of wills still fresh in her mind. It'll be bad enough having to work with the man, without having to share living quarters!

Karen continued on past a dividing line of straight fat bottle trees, and across a stretch of bright, thick green lawn on to a low veranda that surrounded the single-storey brick house. With a total lack of ceremony she pushed open the front door and ushered Jo inside.

'It's all yours,' she said, bowing Jo through the door. 'I'd better get back but if you need anything come on over to the hospital and find me. One of the ward maids was here yesterday giving it a dust and sweep, and I'm sure she left a few basics in the kitchen. Welcome to Warilla, Dr Armitage—in case no one else has done the honours.'

She swept an arm around as if bestowing the rights of all that surrounded them on her companion, and, with a quick grin, departed anxious to complete her work before the next shift arrived to take over.

With a sense of excitement, Jo explored her domain. The main bedroom was to the right, with a smaller bedroom on the left. The short passageway led into a room that was a combined lounge and dining-room, and, through these, she found a functional kitchen, a small laundry and a bathroom. Solid, basic, public service housing, she decided, practical, comfortable but entirely lacking in style. With that judgement, a great yawn reminded her just how tired she was, and, forgetting the shower she had longed for all night, she made straight for the bedroom and collapsed on the bed, pausing only to drag the light cotton bedcover over her legs against the slight chill in the dawn air.

'Oh, for heaven's sake,' an exasperated voice was saying.

The words reverberated in her subconscious for a while, until she realised they were not part of a dream. She dragged herself out of a deep sleep, and opened her eyes.

The voice's owner blocked the doorway—completely! Unless all the men west of the Great Divide were six-four and broad as axe handles, it was Dr Steve Hemming—still disapproving, it seemed!

Jo pushed herself upright on the bed, and rubbed a hand through her hair, trying desperately to shake herself awake in order to cope with this intrusion.

'Were you up all night?' he barked, and she nodded, puzzled by his tone. After all, he was the one who had insisted she remain with the child—wasn't he? She frowned as she tried to put together the sequence of events that had followed her arrival at Warilla.

'I presume that's your car still parked at the front door of the hospital?'

Again she nodded. Had this man woken her to complain about where her car was parked?

'Give me the keys and I'll get one of the men to drive it round for you, then I'll be back. We've got a lot to sort out.'

He held out his hand, a hint of impatience in the motion. Car keys? Jo thought, then remembered an irritating discomfort during her slumbers. She stood up off the bed, and felt in her pocket, pulling out the small bundle of keys. As she moved towards the door to hand them over, she saw the look on her colleague's face, and realised that she was still in her travelling gear.

Steve Hemming was staring at her with a puzzled frown on his face, his eyes moving from her bare brown toes to the top of her sleep-rumpled dark head.

'Oh, for heaven's sake!' he repeated, then vanished out of her doorway.

She shook her head, bemused by his reaction. What she needed was a shower, not to mention a toothbrush, and clean clothes! She would have to wait for the car. There was a towel in her overnight bag on the back seat, she remembered, so she needn't unpack everything before showering. She heard the car pull up at the back of the house and a cheery voice called out, 'I'll leave the keys on the veranda!'

Thankful that no more staff members would see her in this state of dishevelment, she waited a few minutes before retrieving her bag and heading gratefully into the bathroom.

The water was lukewarm, and smelt peculiar, but it cleansed and refreshed, restoring Jo's natural optimism and reviving the spirit of adventure that had accompanied her on the long journey west. Pulling a clean pair of knee-length shorts and matching shirt out of the bottom of the bag, she dressed, combed her hair and emerged, crossing the hall to discover Steve Hemming, very much at home in her small kitchen as he presided over a sizzling pan of bacon and eggs.

Jo stopped in her tracks, staring at the broad back in its blue cotton shirt. There was something about this man that rattled her. Was it simply that he had the experience she lacked? Or that he was a foot taller and looked dependable whereas she looked like a kid who'd strayed into a grown-ups' game?

She shrugged aside the thoughts, mentally blaming tiredness for this uncharacteristic insecurity.

'That smells good,' she said brightly. 'Much better than an olive-branch would, I'm sure.'

He spun around at the sound of her voice, and his heavy-lidded eyes probed questioningly.

'Olive-branch?'

'Peace offering,' she explained.

'Peace offering?' he queried blankly. 'Why on earth should I have to proffer a peace offering?'

Because you behaved so rudely last night! she thought crossly, unable to believe that the man did not realise how inhospitable his 'welcome' had been.

'It was a joke,' she said shortly, stepping over to the bench to fill the kettle and put it on to boil for a much needed cup of coffee.

'Oh!'

With this unsatisfactory response, he turned back to the stove and proceeded to serve up two plates of breakfast fare, despite the fact that it was closer to lunchtime.

'I'll have tea; there are bags in the jar next to the coffee,' he informed her, putting the two plates on the table, already set with cutlery, bread and butter and a small jug of milk.

Stifling an urge to tell him to get it himself—he had, after all, cooked breakfast—Jo made tea and coffee then joined him at the table. As she picked up her knife and fork she looked across at this man whose very presence seemed to incite her to rebel.

His head was bent over his plate and his thick hair was ruffled, untidily cut and barely combed. It always would be, she thought, recognising an urgency in him that gave little time to what he would consider inessentials. The skin on his strong, long-fingered hands and thick bare forearms was tanned, the skin of a man who spent long hours outdoors, rather than the normal pallor of most medical men she knew in the city.

'Eat,' he ordered, looking up from his plate for an instant, his hooded gaze catching her eyes, but revealing nothing. 'I haven't much time and we've got to talk.'

Suppressing various mutinous replies, Jo began to eat, then found hunger overcoming all other considerations. Across from her, the man-mountain polished off his snack and pushed his plate aside, raising his head to study Jo as she finished her meal.

'The fact is, Dr Armitage,' he began in a firm, even, unemotional tone, as she savoured the last mouthfuls with an unsuspecting pleasure, 'your father may have got you this job in Warilla, but I'm the one who decides if you stay here.'

CHAPTER TWO

A BURNING, seething resentment welled up in Jo, and she stifled the urge to hurl her coffee-cup at this insolent, autocratic pig! Literally biting her tongue to prevent her anger spilling out, she schooled her face to a look of blank enquiry and raised her eyes to his. Let him explain his statement! She was damned if she would help him, or encourage further insults by opening her mouth to deny his assumption.

For a moment it seemed like a stalemate. His eyes, blue as the summer sky that shimmered outside the window, challenged hers, daring her to respond. She met his look and held it, refusing to give in — to look away — but, when he finally shifted uneasily in his seat, then sighed, and rubbed his hand through his untidy hair, she knew it was a hollow victory! They should have met as friends, she realised, as colleagues with a common interest and the bond of their profession.

'It's only a temporary appointment, after all,' he said, breaking the silence between them and shaking his head as if to echo her feeling of regret. 'You may have heard that I've been lobbying for an extra doctor to be appointed to this town for the past two years. Regionalisation of the health department in this area has meant more office workers and less services for the people.'

Despite the words, directed at the department which was headed by her father, the venom had gone from his voice and he spoke with a quiet acceptance of the inadequacies of bureaucracy.

'I actually left the public service two years ago, thinking they would replace me at the hospital. I figured that, by setting up in private practice, I would be providing the area with the extra doctor the growing population needs.'

'What happened?' she asked quietly, prompting him to fill in the gaps.

'They decided the hospital didn't need a doctor! Yaroona is three hours down the road. It has the flying surgeons based there as well as a superintendent, registrar and good facilities for practically everything.'

'But that's ridiculous! According to Rosie, Warilla has grown to a population of four thousand over the last two years. She says there are more schoolteachers and even an extra policeman in town, because it's growing so fast! And what good's a flying surgeon in the middle of the night when four accident victims come in?'

'Exactly!' was the dry reply, and Jo looked up, then felt a hot flood of colour mount to her face when she saw the sardonic expression in those blue eyes. 'It took two years to make them see sense, and now——'

'Now you've been stuck with me, and for some reason you feel I'm inadequate,' she said calmly, keeping a tight rein on the anger that had again threatened to erupt, 'despite the fact that I was on the rural medicine programme for two years before I went into research, and have been accepted back on to it.'

Taking a deep breath, she stretched her lips in a semblance of a smile and added sweetly, 'You are obviously glad that this appointment is only temporary, Dr Hemming, but let me assure you that you can't be nearly as glad as I am. The prospect of sharing a workload on a permanent basis with a self-righteous, judgemental know-all like you would be enough to put me off medicine for life.'

A quick glance at the stunned expression on his face told her that the words had hit home, and she felt a fleeting satisfaction. Taking advantage of his silence, she continued, 'Now, perhaps you'd like to tell me a little about the running of the hospital and put forward your suggestions for duty hours, and other practicalities. I am here to work, after all.'

The big man opened and shut his mouth. It was a nice mouth, Jo decided, with even white teeth gleaming behind well-modelled lips—full lips that held a hint of sensuality at odds with his craggy masculinity. His beard was probably darker than his hair, she thought, noting the shadow beneath the smoothly shaven skin. She sat, deliberately forcing herself to relax while she let her eyes rove over a square jawline and stubbornly thrusting chin.

'As you know, it's a twenty-bed hospital,' he told her. 'We have two of those beds taken up by people who would be in a nursing home in a larger town. Allan Walker is an old fellow with emphysema. He's managed fairly well on his own up till now, but has had a series of acute bronchial infections.'

'Is he on a respirator?'

'No, but he's here in case he needs one urgently. I don't want to use it because he could become reliant on it. We use intravenous drugs, aminophylline, corticosteroids and antibiotics in a nice cocktail. Most importantly, we can boost his liquid intake and control his oxygen therapy while he's here.'

'He can't do that at home?'

The words slipped out, and she did not need his answering scowl to tell her she had made another mistake, questioning his decision!

'Of course he can,' came the gravelly reply. 'He boosts his liquid intake with whisky and coffee, and controls his oxygen by puffing at it between cigarettes! Mary Jackson uses the other bed.'

He said no more and she dared not ask. She'd find out about Mary Jackson for herself!

'Monday to Friday there's an outpatients' clinic at nine,' he continued just as the silence between them threatened to become uncomfortable. The words were clipped as he disseminated the information she had asked for without a trace of emotion or involvement.

'You're on call for Casualty twenty-four hours a day when you're on duty. I don't mind coming in for an emergency any time. Thursday's the quietest day so if you take the afternoon and evening off I'll be on call for you then and every second weekend so you get a proper break. If you want me to cover for you any time you're going out of town, or need a good night's sleep, just ask; I'll be happy to fill in.'

The words carried a cold aggression that chilled her soul, but she refused to be intimidated by his rudeness.

'Outpatient work will probably decrease dramatically now that you're offering a private alternative. I imagine most of the townspeople consider you their GP already.'

It was her own olive-branch, as she sought to regain some common ground, to reach some plateau on which they could coexist—if not in harmony, at least in mutual accord!

'You still have to provide the service,' he said with a grating abruptness, and Jo stared at him in blank amazement.

What had happened to cause this antagonism? Was it directed against her father, as head of the department that had refused to listen to his pleas for staff? No,

Colin Armitage had only been in the job three months, and it had been one of his first official decrees that had ensured all twenty-bed hospitals have a medical officer.

She shook her head as she watched him sipping at his tea. It couldn't be to do with her father, yet there was something personal in his attitude towards her, something she could not pin down, but knew was there with an inexplicable certainty. It was a shame, she thought, sighing regretfully, then wondered at her reaction!

'I'll be at the hospital for a few hours, finishing up some paperwork, then on call for the day, and tonight. You start tomorrow,' he said, rising to his feet and stalking out of the room, his footsteps echoing on the polished linoleum in the hallway, and out across the wooden veranda.

What an aggravating, infuriating, bad-tempered bear of a man, Jo thought, as she cleared the table and washed the dishes, checking the cupboards to see where things were kept and noting the supplies some kind person had left on the shelves.

In spite of the company, the meal had heartened her, and she unpacked the car, putting away her clothes, and carefully placing the cushions, pictures and ornaments she had brought with her to give the house a touch of home. This job done, she looked around with pride.

'All it needs is a few flowers,' she told the picture of her parents that rested on the sideboard, and, grabbing a pair of surgical scissors from the cutlery drawer, she went out to explore her yard.

Once off the veranda, the summer heat struck her like a physical blow, pressing down on her bare head, and burning into her skin. A sprinkler was clicking rhythmically as it sprayed water across the lawn—bore water creating an oasis of green in this dry brown land. Bricked garden beds showed where flowers had once grown, but they were choked with weeds. Avoiding the jets of water, she crossed to the bloated bottle trees and reached up to break off three bunches of leaves, admiring the hard black seed pods that clung between their glossy green. An angry buzzing alarmed her, and she looked down to see a bee caught in a bit of web inside one of the pods. Using the point of her scissors, she eased the struggling creature out of the shell, then looked away as a voice called to her.

Rosie was coming towards her from the hospital grounds, and she waved her free hand, feeling, as she did so, the sharp jab of a sting on the inside of her wrist. Almost immediately the pain turned to a burning sensation, and she saw an angry red swelling spreading up her arm.

'I'll pull the sting,' Rosie was saying, but her voice was coming from far away and Jo fought to control her panic. It must be shock, she assured herself—a strange reaction because I'm tired. For some reason, it was becoming harder to breathe and it took all her concentration to get across to the veranda with Rosie's supporting arm.

'Get Dr Hemming,' she managed to wheeze. 'Tell him allergic to bee sting!'

The awful truth had dawned slowly. She had treated many people for anaphylactic shock, but it had never occurred to her that she might be one of a small minority who reacted so violently to insect venom. She sat on the step and breathed carefully, wondering if she should walk across to the hospital and find the drug she needed herself.

In her mind's eye, she could see the textbook description of her reaction and read the words: Administer 1:1000 adrenalin subcutaneously, and watch the patient for signs of further deterioration. Where were the drugs kept?

Her eyes felt hot and itchy, and her eyelids closed slowly with a swelling puffiness.

'Doctors with known allergic reactions should keep antigens handy,' that unwelcome voice was saying sternly. 'I trust you're not pregnant?'

Jo shook her head, then felt her arm lifted and the jab of a hypodermic, but some last remnant of pride forced her to argue.

'Didn't know!' she muttered defensively.

'Hush now!' the voice said, softer and more amiable now — hardly grating at all!

She felt strong arms go around her and she was lifted into the air and cradled against a broad chest.

'Hush now,' Steve Hemming repeated soothingly, carrying her into the house as easily as if she were a baby and lowering her on to the bed with infinite care. He must have pulled back the bedspread, for now he covered her carefully and remained beside the bed, one hand holding her wrist as he took her pulse and examined the still angry redness of the sting.

'I'll get something for that,' he told her. 'Just rest; you'll be OK now.'

She was prepared to believe him, for her breathing had eased miraculously already, although her lips and tongue still felt bloated and her eyes would not open properly.

He was back within minutes, spraying the soothing lotion on to her still swollen wrist.

'How did it happen?' he asked quietly, perhaps to check her speech patterns.

'The bee was caught in the pod,' she explained. 'I was rescuing it.'

'Rescuing a bee?'

'Yes,' she said defiantly. 'I hate to see things die!'

'It would have died after stinging you anyway,' he pointed out with irrefutable logic.

Hot, heavy tears welled up in her eyes. She was tired, and far from home, and this man was saying she'd killed the bee.

'You're not crying, are you?' he demanded suspiciously.

'Of course I'm not,' she said, sniffing hopelessly as a tear rolled down her cheek.

'Oh, for heaven's sake,' he muttered.

It must be his favourite way of expressing disgust, Jo thought, but the misery of her situation continued to overwhelm her and other tears followed.

'Surely all of this emotion isn't about a dead bee?' he asked, the exasperation in his voice detracting from the comfort his arms were offering as he lowered his great bulk on to the bed and slid a hand under her shoulders, lifting her against his massive chest.

'I hate to kill things, even ants,' she muttered, 'but I don't usually cry about it. I must be very tired.' She gave another sniff and felt the pressure of his arm tighten around her shoulders. His body radiated a heat that warmed her, and she fought an urge to snuggle closer, to seek oblivion from her present problems in those arms.

My mind must be wandering, she thought, shocked by her body's reaction to this man. He's the problem, not the solution! she told herself sternly.

'I'd advise you to get over this little fancy of yours.' The words had a hard edge, his voice as cool as his arms were warm. 'Out here, it's often a case of kill or be killed, and stupidity ——'

'Like rescuing a bee!'

'Exactly! Stupidity like rescuing a bee could lead to death.'

His words hit her like a bucket of cold water, shaking her out of her fantasy about security in his arms.

'Aren't you over-dramatising it just a little?' she asked, annoyed that he could upset her so easily but hiding her hurt behind the unsubtle sarcasm.

'No! If you'd been anywhere but fifty yards from the hospital, your stupidity could have killed you. Don't you see that? And out here it's not just bees—there are ants that would probably affect you the same way, and wasps and hornets—and that's just the insect world. How are you going to handle snakes?'

She shuddered uncontrollably, then pushed herself away from his body, turning to face him on the bed.

'I shall run for my life or die of heart failure when I see the snake, so there's no worry about dying of snake-bite,' she explained in a flat, matter-of-fact voice. 'I have a phobia about snakes. Even looking at pictures of them in books fills me with fear and loathing, and it's no good saying that I should get over it, because I've tried and I can't.'

Talking about them made her shiver and squirm, and she saw the look of disdain on Steve Hemming's face as he watched her reaction with a detached, almost scientific interest.

'Didn't you think about snakes before you came rushing out here to minister to the sick in the bush?'

'Of course I did. I simply thought it unlikely that I'd encounter any of them, walking the short distance from the house to the hospital and back.'

'There's more to rural medicine than hospital duty,' he said harshly, obviously upset by her flippant attitude.

'What do you mean?' she demanded, the antagonism he could stir so easily burning inside her.

'I mean that the local doctor is part of the community, and should be involved with it. For too long doctors were posted to these places against their will—to work out the terms of a scholarship or because there were no other jobs. Some of them were great, some stayed on, but others came and sat here thinking, like you, that all they had to do was administer the hospital for a short time, then leave.'

That he believed passionately in what he was saying Jo had no doubt. His conviction was written in every line of his taut body, and in the frowning concentration in his eyes as he sought for words to explain his belief. Was it his certainty that he was always right that she found so aggravating? Whatever it was, she felt compelled to argue.

'What harm could they possibly do, providing they performed their job to everyone's satisfaction?'

'Doing a job efficiently and being a good doctor are two entirely different things,' he told her. 'Half the battle in healing is trust, and if you don't realise that you shouldn't be here. If patients trust you they believe you, and if they believe they'll get better, then most of the time they will, but without that trust in the first place you get nowhere!'

It was a familiar argument, and one she had used numerous times herself, especially when she defended her decision to wear coloured coats—believing that sterile white coats held doctors apart from their patients and reinforced the barriers between them. However, while she might agree in principle, her battling spirit was not yet ready to concede this, or any other debate, to Steve Hemming.

She opened her mouth to make a point, but the man was not finished.

'Trust isn't something that's handed out with medical degrees, you know. It has to be won, and sitting in splendid isolation behind the walls of this complex is not the way to win it!'

He stood up as he spoke, and finished his lecture glaring down at her.

'I've got work to do; I'll call back later and check on you. In the meantime, get some sleep,' he ordered, then strode out of the room.

'Oh, for heaven's sake!' Jo muttered, picking up on the catchphrase.

She sank back down on to the pillows, her body trembling with anger and indignation and her head aching dully as her body continued to battle with the poison and medication.

She woke in a lather of sweat, the heat of the day having penetrated the cool brick building. Another tepid shower made her feel better, but the dry heat seemed to burn through her within minutes of emerging from it. Pulling on a light cotton sundress, she decided to walk across to the hospital and visit the Andrews family. Although not officially on duty, she felt she could justify a friendly visit as she had attended to them in the first place. It would also be air-conditioned over there, and feeling cool was becoming a high priority.

There was a motherly-looking cook on duty in the big kitchen and a delicious aroma of baked biscuits hung in the air. Jo introduced herself, receiving a friendly welcome from Mrs Melrose, and explained her mission.

'The little girl's as bright as a button,' the older woman assured her. 'She's been in here with me half

the day. Shouldn't really be in hospital, but what can
you do? They're southerners, on holiday up this way.'

Jo smiled. Mrs Melrose could probably tell her what
colour their house was and the name of their next-door
neighbour, hospital gossip being what it was!

'I'll go and visit them, and see you on my way out,'
she said, wondering what happened to children in cases
like this, when the parents were likely to be incapaci-
tated for some time, and all their friends and family
were far away.

Mrs Andrews was thinking along the same lines! Her
eyes were on the doorway when Jo entered the ward,
nodding to two other patients she had seen briefly the
night before.

'Oh, Doctor,' she greeted Jo. 'I'm so glad you called
in. I've seen Jenny, of course, and I know she's fine,
but what's going to happen to her? Will she be able to
stay here until we can travel? Do you think that would
be best? I'm worried about what she might see, or that
she might get into trouble, or be in the way!'

'You've obviously been upsetting yourself by thinking of every possible mischief she can get up to!' Jo
scolded, smiling cheerfully to hide her own concern
about the child. 'You're the patient and patients aren't
supposed to worry. They leave all that to their doctor!'

Her light words won a slight response, as her
patient's lips twisted into a smile, and some of the
concern left her shadowed eyes.

'I live here in the hospital grounds, so she can always
stay with me until you're fit to be released. It will only
be a day or two before your ankle settles down and
you're able to get about. Before we decide, I'll speak
to Matron, and see if she knows a nice family in town
with children about Jenny's age. If they would take her
in, I'm certain you'd feel easier about her, and she

would have other kids to play with and plenty to keep her occupied.'

'That's a wonderful idea,' Kate Andrews replied. 'Do you really think someone would do it?'

'This is the west,' Jo reminded her, sounding far more confident than she felt, considering the idea had only just occurred to her. 'Haven't you heard about western hospitality? Leave it with me, and I'll let you know later how I've got on.'

She moved to the end of the bed, automatically picking up the chart and checking the entries on it.

'Now that we've sorted out Jenny's problems, how are you feeling?'

'My arm's a bit sore still and my ankle is still very swollen, but, apart from that, I'm fine. One of the nurses wheeled me in to see my husband earlier. He says his chest is very painful, but the other doctor told him it's just bruising. He's spoken to a policeman and says the car will be all right!'

He would! Jo thought. It's the only thing he's worried about all along. Stifling the urge to say something cutting about men and their priorities, she smiled encouragingly.

'I'll get on to Matron now, and come back as soon as we've sorted something out,' she said as she turned to leave the ward.

Two hours later, she and Rosie had introduced a charming family to Jenny and her parents and seen the little girl depart happily, and her mother relax contentedly. They sat in Rosie's office, Jo putting off the time when she must return to her little house and think about feeding herself, and Rosie lingered in the hope that her husband would feed their kids if she was late enough.

'That was a great idea,' Rosie praised. 'We do similar

things when a mother goes into labour early and the child-minder she's organised hasn't arrived, but we've never had to arrange things for an outside family like this before.'

'Maybe I will be able to offer something to rural medicine,' she responded ruefully.

'Of course you will. Why should you doubt it?'

'Dr Hemming seems to think my phobia about snakes will make me completely inadequate for the job—especially now I've added bee-sting allergy to my failings.' She could not prevent her bitterness spilling into the words.

'It was too bad about the bee sting,' Rosie said sympathetically. 'Are you feeling OK now? I must admit I was surprised when you arrived earlier; I'd expected you to spend the day in bed.'

'I probably would have if it hadn't got so hot. I really came over here to get into the air-conditioning and cool off!'

'Didn't Steve turn on your air-conditioning? Honestly, anyone would think the man resented your arrival, when he's been after another doctor for this town for years!'

'He might have wanted another doctor, but somehow I don't seem to fit his job description,' Jo said in a small voice, her hard-won confidence deserting her again at the mention of the man who disliked her so much.

'Nonsense,' replied Rosie bracingly. 'Just because you're *petite* and feminine and far too pretty for your own good, he's reacted with the typical male response that you must also be incapable. From what I've heard of your actions last night, you'll soon prove him wrong.'

'I might prove him wrong, but I doubt he'll ever

admit it,' Jo replied with a wry smile. 'He doesn't strike me as a man who backs down easily!'

'Maybe not,' Rosie admitted, rising to her feet reluctantly. 'Come on; I'll walk over with you and show you where the air-conditioning switches are. If you don't want to cook for yourself, Melly will always give you a meal in the kitchen. She'll also tell you everything that's happening in the town while you eat!'

Jo followed her out of the office, through the kitchen and across the brightly lit yard towards her house. A light shone above the door, illuminating the veranda and front steps, and there was the muted hum of machinery coming from behind the house.

'Someone's thought of your comfort,' Rosie told her. 'That noise is your air-conditioner going. If you look on the back veranda, you'll see a control box with the switches.' She paused at the bottom of the shallow steps. 'Do you think you'll be OK?'

'Of course I will,' Jo assured her and watched as her new friend walked back towards the hospital to check on things once more before returning home to her family.

A pleasant glow warmed her as she crossed the veranda and pushed open the door. She had tackled her first problem, and found a solution that made everyone happy, and, although there was nothing miraculous or earth-shattering in what she had done, she felt a quiet sense of achievement.

There were lights on inside her house, and noises coming from the kitchen! She stopped in the doorway, her heart pounding, all her city-bred fear and distrust sharpening her senses. Not only noises, she realised, but a very enticing smell of food! Burglars, murderers and rapists would hardly cook her a meal before attacking her, she decided, and relaxed. It was eight o'clock and she had last eaten at about eleven, when Steve Hemming had fed her bacon and eggs.

'Who's there?' she called, pleased that her voice sounded calm and controlled.

'Hemming!' came the abrupt reply, and the pounding of her heart began again. If the man disliked her so much, why did he keep intruding like this? Why did he keep feeding her?

The aroma from the kitchen was certainly enticing, drawing her reluctantly towards it. 'Don't you have a kitchen of your own to cook in?' she demanded, aware of the belligerence in her voice.

'I actually came over to check on your health, and leave you this,' he replied mildly, indicating an inhaler on the table between them.

'What is it?' she asked suspiciously.

'Adrenalin! Keep it with you at all times, understand, and use two or three puffs immediately after you are stung by anything. You should also take a series of desensitising injections. I could arrange to get the venom if you want to try it.'

'I'll stick with the inhaler for a while,' she said quietly, not knowing quite how to fit this caring side of the man into her previous image of him.

'Suit yourself,' he replied, shrugging his bulky shoulders and turning back to the pan that was spluttering on the stove. 'Dinner in two minutes, OK?'

'That's fine,' she answered weakly, heading for the bathroom as if to escape some danger.

It was less than twenty-four hours since she had arrived in this town, and yet so much had happened! Throughout her long journey, she had repeatedly pictured her arrival, imagining the welcome she might receive and the little courtesies that might be extended to her. How far from those images was the reality!

She splashed cold water on her face, regretting that she had not bothered to put on some make-up before heading for the hospital and its promised coolness. Her skin was clear, but there were dark shadows under her eyes, and the unease she felt in this new world was mirrored in the shadows that deepened her brown eyes to lightless pools of blackness. She brushed her short cap of hair fiercely, enjoying the scrape of the brush against her scalp, then grimaced at her reflection and left the room.

Steve Hemming was opening a bottle of chilled wine, his large, capable hands gleaming wetly from the condensation that beaded the green glass.

'It's an olive-branch,' he said, looking up at her and smiling as he pulled out the cork with a triumphant tug.

Jo felt the ground shift under her feet! It was less a smile than a teasing quirk of his lips, as if he was inviting her to share the joke! She responded with all her natural friendliness, pleased that they seemed to have crossed some hurdle that had lain between them.

'Oh,' she said, smiling back at him with warm cheeks and glowing eyes, 'I'm so glad you said that! I was beginning to think you didn't like me.'

Across the table, Steve finished filling the second glass with wine, concentrating on his task before looking up at her.

'Oh, I don't,' he said, in cordial tones, 'but we are colleagues and we do have to work together, so I thought we'd better establish some kind of truce!'

The effrontery of this bland statement stripped Jo of breath. She could only stand and stare at him, mouth agape as she tried to assimilate what he had just said.

'How dare you say that?' she demanded, when anger burnt through her dismay and lent impetus to her tongue. 'How can you judge someone you don't even know? How can you possibly decide you don't like me? You don't even know me!'

She stamped her foot in indignation, aware that she must look like a small child having a tantrum, but unable to control the rage that flared within her slim frame. She had put up with this man's rudeness since she first arrived at this place, but she would not put up with it any longer. She wanted an explanation of his attitude, and she would get one if it was the last thing she did!

'Are you just against female doctors, or is it all women you dislike? Is it a general prejudice or have I been singled out as the sole object of your disdain?' she spluttered, her fury feeding on itself, and her voice rising shrilly.

Throughout her tirade, the man stood looking down at her without a flicker of emotion on his darkly handsome face. The dinner still simmered on the stove behind him, and the brimming wine glasses remained untouched on the table between them. Tension stretched through the air like electrical currents before a fierce storm and Jo shivered as her anger cooled.

There was something in the very immobility of this man that frightened her, and a chill of apprehension began to replace the heat of anger.

'Martin Collins was my best friend at university,' he said, his lips tight, his eyes bleakly watchful.

The shock of his words froze her mind for an instant, until she realised that she had come a long way to escape this type of pre-judgement.

'So?' Defiance flashed across the space that separated them.

'He came up to stay with me after you dumped him. Told me how you'd treated him—sought to get ahead of him in the research department, using your father's influence to worm your way in with those who handed out the money. He was devastated, all but destroyed. . . We talked—discussed his work. . . I thought I'd given him back some of his hope for the future but I must have failed!'

His head dropped and he banged the table with his fist, making the cutlery ring and clatter.

'But it wasn't like that!' she protested, the words a despairing wail.

'No?' he sneered, raising his head to transfix her with accusing eyes. 'Then why else would a man as brilliant as Martin take his own life?'

Jo felt a surge of nausea, and fled, out across the back veranda, past the car, and the shed where the air-conditioning motor thumped, coming to a halt in the deep shadow of tall gum tree, where she slumped against the trunk and retched uncontrollably.

CHAPTER THREE

SLOWLY, the churning turbulence subsided, and the cooling air wrapped around her as the magic of the night brought its own peace. Through the branches of the tree, she could see the sky, bright with stars that seemed to burn more fiercely out here in the outback, lighting up the darkness with their white radiance.

I must go back inside, she told herself, forcing her mind to think calmly and logically. I must eat, phone my parents to let them know I've arrived, then go to bed so I'm fit to face a new beginning tomorrow.

Could there ever be a new beginning, she wondered, or would this happen whenever she moved? Wherever she went? Would there always be someone who would remember her name and connect it to Martin?

Memory was so selective! she thought dejectedly. No one seemed to remember the other girls Martin had taken out. Nor did they consider that she hadn't seen him for four months before he ended his life in such a spectacular fashion. They looked for a reason why so brilliant a man would take his own life, and found a broken engagement. Who had done the breaking no longer mattered — especially if Martin had given different versions to different people! Two and two making five as usual, she thought, with uncharacteristic bitterness.

Somewhere a phone was ringing. It had to be in her house, she decided, with weary resignation. Let Steve Hemming answer it, she thought, but the jangling noise continued.

I'm a doctor, and doctors always answer phones, she told herself as she pushed reluctantly away from the sheltering trunk and moved stiffly back to the house, treading warily across the veranda and into the now deserted kitchen.

'Did I get you out of bed, or out of the shower?' Rosie's voice was asking in response to her hello.

'I was out the back, communing with nature,' she explained.

'With the snakes?'

'Oh, Rosie, I'd forgotten all about them!' A swift shudder ran through her body, but Rosie diverted her.

'It's very rare you see them around the town,' she assured her, 'especially near the hospital, with all the traffic coming and going, and the gardeners keeping everything in order. I rang to see if you're OK. I'm just off to bed myself, but thought I'd check on you first. After all, you have been a patient today.'

'Thanks, Rosie, I'm fine. One good night's sleep will work wonders. Will you be on duty in the morning?'

'Will I?' was the prompt reply. 'I'll be there with bells on to welcome the new doctor!'

They both laughed, Rosie's friendliness acting like a soothing balm on Jo's bruised spirits.

'See you in the morning, then,' Jo answered, replacing the receiver with a grin.

She looked around the kitchen. Apart from the lingering smell of food, it was as if Steve Hemming had never been there. The table was cleared, the glasses and plates put away. Puzzled, she opened the refrigerator door and found the corked bottle of wine, and a casserole dish containing the dinner he had cooked. An irritating sense of guilt crept over her, but she pushed it aside. He might have come seeking peace, but, if that was the case, why did he deliberately bait her? Why tell her, with such cool contempt, that he didn't like her? Why taunt her with memories of Martin?

Bother the man, she thought angrily. He's not even here, and he's still upsetting me!

With a grim determination she filled the kettle and switched it on, found some bread and made herself an unappetising sandwich of cold casserole, then dialled her parents' number.

'I'm an Armitage,' she said aloud, as she listened to the phone ringing in that familiar home thousands of miles away, 'and Armitages can do *anything*!'

'What are you doing this weekend?' Melly asked, as Jo sat in the kitchen reviving herself with a cup of coffee.

'I haven't given it a thought,' she replied. 'To tell you the truth, the last two weeks have passed so quickly, I can't quite believe I'm due for proper time off.'

'You've settled in just great,' Melly assured her. 'The whole town's talking about how good you are!'

'Oh, Melly, that's just nonsense and you know it,' she said, smiling in spite of herself. 'The "whole town's" barely aware that I exist, and it's either very healthy or they're all going to Dr Hemming. They probably don't trust a female doctor!'

'Oh, we've had a female doctor once before,' Melly declared, surprising Jo with the information. 'Hilary Waring, a friend of Steve's. Did a locum for three months while he was on a course. She still comes out quite often. We used to think she and Steve might get married one day but——'

'Whoa there!' Jo threw up her hands. 'I'm quite happy to listen to all your tall tales about the inhabitants of this town, mainly because I don't know any of them and probably never will, but I draw the line at hospital gossip, Melly. I hate my friends talking about me when I'm not with them, so I refuse to do it to others!'

'It's hardly gossip to tell you something you'll find out for yourself before very long!' There was a defensive note in Melly's pleasant country voice, and Jo responded to it with a chuckle.

'Let me wait and find out the worst!' she said, then added quickly, 'Tell me, then, if it isn't an aversion to female doctors that keeps the townsfolk away from me, is it something personal, like my coloured coats or because I'm too short?'

Melly laughed at the nonsense, her indignation forgotten.

'Seriously, Melly, all I've seen in the fortnight has been the man with the tropical ulcer, who comes in for a fresh dressing each day, and the most junior nurse could handle that —'

'But she couldn't clean out the wound, or prescribe antibiotic powder or the medicated bandages — you have to be there!'

'And if I wasn't you could probably do it — Spersin powder and Sofra Tulle, that's all you'd need,' Jo told her, laughing at Melly's flow of medical knowledge. 'And treat the odd burnt foot, gastro case, and stitch up the lacerations from the pub brawls!'

'Don't you believe it, and don't worry about people not liking you. Outpatients is never very busy. Folks out here don't like to bother the doctor for little things!'

'Perhaps that's just as well! With the spate of car accidents we've had, there's been more than enough to keep me occupied!'

'Which brings me back to my question. Do you have anything planned for the weekend?'

'Apart from sleeping, cleaning my house, doing the washing, sleeping, writing some letters, shopping and more sleeping, no!'

The older woman laughed. 'You should get out and see a bit of the country,' she scolded.

'If there's no big drama to keep me here, I'll take you out to my place.'

Jo stiffened at the sound of the voice. She had seen Steve every day since she began work, passing him in the wards when he came in to visit his private patients, discussing people who had been in his care before she arrived, assisting him in operations when the two of them were required for minor surgery or patching up the accident victims that had trickled steadily through the door.

With rigid control, she had erected a cool, efficient, indifferent façade, and took refuge behind it whenever he appeared. Her professionalism ensured that she did what was required of her with thorough expertise, but to him she revealed nothing of the warm and caring human being that the patients and other staff were beginning to know.

'I was just telly Melly that I'll be too busy for sightseeing this weekend,' she replied calmly, draining the last of her coffee with a gulp and rising from her chair.

'If you change your mind, the hospital will know where to find me,' he said shortly. 'Now, if I can have a few minutes of your time, I'd like to discuss the theatre schedule.'

'Come through to the office.' Her voice sounded coolly confident in her ears, belying the inner queasiness that his presence seemed to generate.

I may be able to put up a good front, she admitted

silently, as her neck prickled with an awareness of his proximity, but inside I'm a quivering mess.

She moved around the desk and sat on the edge of the big leather chair she had inherited from him. It was big enough for three people her size, and made her feel even smaller than she was, but it must be department property or he would have taken it with him when he left.

'Dave Purvis, the flying surgeon, operates here next Wednesday. The third Wednesday of every month is his scheduled day, although, as you know, he'll come for emergencies in between those times.'

He was slumped in the visitor's chair, his face lined with fatigue. One of his private patients had given birth to a fine baby boy in the early hours of the morning, and, from the look of him, he had spent the entire night with her as they awaited the new arrival. Jo dismissed the twinge of concern that distracted her thoughts momentarily.

'I've sorted out the public patients,' she said. 'Two of them have been into Outpatients for appointments, and Julie has contacted the others to let them know they'll have to come in the night before.' She ruffled through the papers on her desk and pushed the list across to him. 'I've listed Mr Grant's arthroscopy first — it should be the simplest — then the Cartwright child's tonsillectomy. As you recommended the operation to his parents, would you like to assist on that one?'

He nodded. 'Poor little blighter was sick all through last winter, right up until Christmas really. We tried preventative doses of penicillin, but even that didn't work.' His eyes travelled down the list. 'Gastroscopy for Mrs Manners — yes, her haemoglobin level is very low — ten grams per hundred millilitres, and I've tried iron supplements and B12 injections. I'm sure there's bleeding somewhere but it's not showing in the faeces. I wondered about polyps in the stomach and spoke to Dave on the phone.'

He looked up from the list and she felt an unspoken thought hovering in the air, unsettling her professional equilibrium.

'Do you have any private patients to add to the list?' she asked, bringing her mind firmly back to the task in hand.

'Just one exploratory,' Steve said vaguely as if his mind was grappling with something to which there was no answer. 'I think!' he added, scratching his head and rubbing his hand across his forehead as if to make his brain work better.

'There's a problem?'

'When isn't there?' he groaned, sounding almost human as he battled with his doubts.

'Can you talk about it?' she asked in her most matter-of-fact voice which hid the anxiety that his mood was causing her. He was always so capable, so much in control, that she found this new, uncertain colleague very disturbing.

'It's an old fellow, Josh Evans. He's lived out here all his life. Worked on Cooraminya for fifty years then retired to a little place on the edge of town.'

Jo sat in silence, letting him feel his way to the words he needed to explain his dilemma.

'A lot of these older people won't "bother the doctor" until it's too late,' he went on, unknowingly echoing the words that Melly had used earlier. 'I'm pretty sure he's got bowel cancer, although we've done a colonoscopy and found nothing.' He shook his head in frustration, one hand running through his already untidy hair. 'I don't know what else it could be — all the signs are there.'

'What usually happens in doubtful cases like this?'

'The surgeon does an exploratory, and, depending on what we find, he either sends them over to Rockhampton for further surgery and post-op treatment, or. . .'

'Or sews them up again because it's too late?' Her voice reflected the sympathy she felt for the patients who were treated this way, receiving a death sentence when all they were looking for was hope.

'Yes,' he said gruffly, reluctantly acknowledging the limitations of modern medicine.

'Is that what's worrying you about Mr Evans? Are you afraid it's too far advanced to do anything?'

He looked up at her with a puzzled frown, as if wondering who was talking to him. Under the heavy lids, there was anguish in those blue eyes, and, for the first time, Jo warmed towards this man who felt so deeply for his patients.

'I'm more afraid of the other diagnosis,' he told her ruefully, his beautiful lips curving upwards in a slight smile. 'I can't send him to Rocky,' he explained. 'It would kill him, not cure him! He's a quiet old codger, but he knows everyone in town and they know him. Here, he's among friends — while over there, no matter how kind people are, he'd be surrounded by strangers and pine away.'

'Maybe you're worrying unnecessarily. Plenty of bowel tumours are removable, even if it means a colostomy. If an exploratory shows it to be something else, people have had chemotherapy administered in their homes, so surely we can arrange with a good oncologist and do it all here by remote control.'

Did she imagine a lightening of the tension in that

suntanned face? It was usually like a mask of carved teak when it turned towards her, but she fancied she detected a slight softening!

'It would be extra work for you,' he said stiffly. 'He would need more care than I could give privately so, although I'd give you all the help I can, he'd still be your responsibility.'

'Worried I won't be able to cope, Dr Hemming?' she asked very quietly.

'No,' he muttered. 'I'm damn sure you'll be able to cope, if only to prove something to me!' He waved his arms in the air in a gesture that suggested surrender, and added, 'You're an extremely competent doctor, but I don't think I ever doubted you would be. It's in your blood, after all!'

Why, thank you, Dr Hemming, she thought, hugging the back-handed compliment tightly to herself.

'It'll mean a long day in Theatre as well,' he warned, and she nodded, knowing that it would mean an even longer day for her and the nursing staff, as they coped with the post-operative patients.

With rare accord, they turned back to the list, dividing up the assisting jobs between them.

At times like this, Jo thought, I realise how pleasant life in this town could be, working in quiet harmony with another professional and seeing the results of that work all around you in the town. How many medical practitioners would know their patients as people, to the extent that a country doctor does?

'I have a property about half an hour out of town. I spend most of my time out there, even when I'm on call. I'd be happy to show you around.'

Had he also felt the appeal of the common bond between them? This sounded like yet another olive-branch! It was a bad comparison, she decided as the thought provoked memories of their last attempt at social intercourse.

'I need a restful weekend,' she repeated, then almost immediately regretted the words as the thought of two days with no duty—no human contact—stretched before her. 'Perhaps some other time,' she added.

'Perhaps!' he said, with a strange inflexion in his voice. 'No doubt I'll see you Monday.'

With that, he was on his feet and gone, moving so lightly and quietly for a man of his size that she could amost believe he had dematerialised.

She was still staring at the open doorway when another head appeared.

'Got a minute?' Karen asked.

Jo nodded, bringing her mind back to everyday matters that did not include mountainous men!

'I've just had a call from my brother. He's been in Mount Isa for the last two years, working for the mines, and is passing through this weekend on his way back to Brisbane. He's going to stay—probably to check up on little sister—and I wondered. . .'

'Does he need accommodation?' Jo knew that Karen shared a flat in town with two male schoolteachers.

'No. . .'

'I refuse to play twenty questions,' she teased. 'Just ask!'

'I know you're off duty this weekend and I wondered if you'd come out to dinner with us tonight,' Karen begged, her hands twisting anxiously as she spoke. 'I want him to meet Bob but I don't want Bob to feel he's being inspected by the family, or be intimidated or anything,' she finished lamely.

Jo smiled, appreciating Karen's concern. From what she had told Jo, her relationship with Bob, the new young policeman in town, was still in its early stages, and Jo could understand her reluctance to put it under too much strain.

'Anything to help true love find its way!' she joked. 'Where, and when, and what does one wear to go out in Warilla?'

'All the hotels have dining-rooms but I reckon Brian will want something more up-market and the only really posh place to eat in Warilla is the Golf Club,' Karen replied earnestly. 'Friday and Saturday nights they even have a band! I'll talk to him when he gets here, and we'll collect you at about seven. Wherever we go, I'll wear a dress. People like getting dressed up in this town, even if it's only to go down to the pub for dinner!'

Karen laughed as she said it, but Jo could hear an echo of regret behind the light-hearted words. Dressed in her neat blue sister's uniform, Karen still managed to look fashionable. She would have loved to go out to places where people dressed in the latest trends, and sported the newest hairstyles.

'I'll see you at seven,' she promised, inwardly determined that, for Karen's sake, she would make an effort to look her very best.

Brian Short was a very charming rascal, she had decided by eight o'clock as they sat on the veranda of the Golf Club, her hunger relieved by an entrée of fresh-water crayfish, and her tiredness dissipated by the icily cold chardonnay she sipped cautiously.

'Perhaps you'd better explain what connection there is between meteorology — which I take to be the study of the weather — and mines.'

'I'd far rather explain my theory about why women with pansy brown eyes and pouty red lips invariably fall in love with me!'

'Meteorology first,' she insisted, pushing away a hand that kept creeping up her arm.

There was a pause while the young waitress refilled their glasses.

I suppose from Karen's point of view I'm doing a good job, Jo thought. I've certainly diverted Brian's attention away from Bob. She cast a despairing glance across the table, but the other pair were lost in a world of their own.

'Why do mines need a weather man?' she repeated, as they settled back to wait for their next course.

'It's not so much the mines, but the initial processing of the ore that is done at the site,' Brian explained, speaking in a soft seductive voice and running the tip of one finger up the back of her hand. 'It gives off noxious sulphur dioxide fumes, and the entire town depends on yours truly to keep their air pure and breatheable.'

Jo chuckled.

'Having asked the question, I don't know whether to believe the answer or not!'

'It's true,' Brian protested. 'I'm a man of power in Mount Isa. With one push of a button, I can stop the mines — which are the sole reason for the town's existence.'

'Oh, yes?' she teased, pleased to have diverted him from his harmless but irritating flirtation.

'Certainly,' he said with great dignity. 'The weather blows up from the south-west, with low level cloud that traps the fumes, and if little Brian doesn't blow the whistle then the whole town is poisoned!'

His finger had stopped its stroking but his hand lay possessively on top of hers.

'Enjoying your time off, Dr Armitage?'

The question echoed through her body, the rumbled

words reverberating in her bones. She snatched her hand away from Brian's, and spun around.

'Very much,' she said lightly, looking up at Steve with a challenging smile. 'We were just discussing the weather in Mount Isa. Do you know Karen's brother Brian?'

She was prattling! She knew that, but the man's sudden appearance had disturbed her and she could feel the tension that his presence always caused building up. Fortunately, Karen took over the introductions, and by the time they were complete the main meal had arrived.

'Are you meeting friends or would you like to join us?' Karen was asking him, oblivious to a furious glare from her brother.

'Thanks, Karen, but I'm just here for a quick bite. I had a long night last night and felt too lazy to cook for myself. Enjoy yourselves,' he added in a general farewell as he walked across to a vacant table by the windows that looked into the bar and dance-floor.

Brian's explanation of his importance to Mount Isa continued, but Jo found it hard to concentrate on the words, or to appreciate the juicy tender steak that she had ordered. She was no longer relaxed, and an enervating weariness was creeping over her as the pleasant conviviality of the evening lost its power to hold her tiredness at bay.

'Dance with me, pretty doctor?' Brian asked as their empty plates were removed.

With a curious reluctance, Jo rose to her feet. More than anything she wanted to be at home in her bed but she had agreed to come and could not spoil the evening for the others. The only thing that did please her was that she had taken the trouble to get dressed up.

As she walked with Brian to the small dance-floor

inside the clubhouse, she felt the swish of silk chiffon against her legs, and knew that the creamy-coloured material, with its sprays of bright flowers, suited her to perfection. The dress was simply cut, with narrow shoulder-straps showing off her lightly tanned shoulders. The rounded neckline hinted at the fullness of her breasts and the gored cut emphasised her tiny waist and slender hips, then flared to a fullness around her calves, giving her an illusion of height that few clothes could achieve.

She could not see what others saw — hair that formed a shining cap to frame her delicately moulded face, carefully darkened eyebrows and lashes emphasising the brilliance of her sparkling eyes, a pert nose that relieved the coldness of classical beauty, and a wide, full mouth that smiled easily, pressing dimples into her delicately flushing cheeks — but as she moved into Brian's arms she was confident that she looked her best and was irrationally pleased that Dr Hemming was there to observe it!

The rhythm of the music enticed her feet, and her body swayed to the tune. She closed her mind to everything except the movement, accepting Brian's whispered flow of compliments as she accepted the medley of sounds around her. She circled the floor with the other dancers, a stranger in their midst, and felt her tension slowly easing, although the tiredness remained.

When the music ended, she felt cheated. It had been a pleasant interlude. Brian's arm encircled her waist, and she looked quickly across to where Steve had sat, but he was gone, the table empty!

'Coming to Yaroona for the cricket tomorrow?' Bob asked as they returned to their seats.

'You bet,' said Brian, this enthusiastic response almost drowning Jo's quick,

'No way!'

They all laughed, and the talk turned to the match and the possibility of beating the champion side. Although she had little interest in the game, Jo was grateful for its importance when she gathered that Bob was the star bowler and was determined to have an early night before the big challenge.

'Sure you won't come tomorrow?' Brian asked as he walked her to her door less than an hour later.

'Quite sure,' she assured him. 'Driving three hours each way to watch a cricket match may appeal to some, but extra sleep is far more enticing for me.'

'Maybe I'll see you Sunday, then,' he said, giving her a light kiss on the cheek and returning to where Bob and Karen waited in the car.

In spite of a tiredness that felt like a deadly lethargy, Jo's night was unexpectedly restless. She tossed and turned, dozed and woke, the legacy of being on call for a fortnight, when all sleep is taken with a part of the mind alert for interruptions. At three, she made herself a cup of tea and read for a while, until her eyelids drooped, and she finally sank into a deep, undisturbed slumber.

It was ten o'clock before she awoke, feeling refreshed and rejuvenated — with an energy that bubbled and fizzed inside her.

I'll go to town, she decided, as she finished a sketchy breakfast. Walk down, do my shopping, have a cup of coffee at the Fig Tree café that the girls all talk about and ignore the housework until this afternoon.

Slapping a broad-brimmed hat on her head, she grabbed her string bag and headed off, pausing on the veranda to pick up a note that was propped against a pot-plant on the top step.

Opening it, she read as she walked. It was from Karen, suggesting that they collect her at ten the next morning for a swim and picnic out at the weir. Not wanting to wake her at the crack of dawn when they were setting off for Yaroona, they had dropped the note on the doorstep.

Jo smiled. It sounded lovely. Brian was good company, and he would be leaving on Monday, so there would be no complications. Would she shy away from complications forever? she wondered, but even this depressing thought could not suppress the spring in her step, nor the sparkle in her eyes as she set out to explore her new, if temporary home-town.

Rounding the hospital, she admired the bright display of marigolds and calendulas that filled the garden bed in the centre of the circular drive. Steve's big four-wheel-drive station wagon was parked at the front steps. He must be doing his rounds before heading off to his property out of town. She felt a momentary curiosity about his life, but stifled it. Climbing into a pit of snakes would be preferable to getting tangled up with Steve.

'Can I give you a lift?'

The big vehicle must have coasted down the drive, for she hadn't heard a sound. He was leaning across the seat, his tawny head half out of the window, looking down at her as she stood by the side of the road. She tried to read his eyes, but they hid his thoughts too well.

It's too nice a day for quarrels, she decided, her pleasure in the day still warming her eyes and twisting her lips into a happy smile.

'I'm just going into town — to the supermarket,' she told him.

'I'm going that way,' he replied gravely.

Much as she wanted to walk, it would be churlish to refuse. Somehow, all the overtures towards peace that either of them made turned sour and they ended up having an argument. She would try once more, she decided, but only because she was in such a good mood.

'OK,' she said and reached up to grab the door as it opened. It seemed a long way up, and, once there, she was grateful that the cabin was so spacious. There was plenty of room between herself and this man who seemed determined to disrupt her life — one way or another.

'Did you know Brian Short before?' he asked as she settled herself in her seat. There was a thrusting combativeness in his voice that made Jo immediately regret her decision to accept the lift.

'No,' she responded warily, her eyes on his unrevealing profile as he stared straight out at the road ahead. 'Karen asked me to join them for dinner.'

'I did wonder,' he murmured, his voice expressionless, 'because there are so few women these days foolish enough to take a man home with them on their first date.'

'What *are* you talking about?' Jo asked with a puzzled frown, her mood still buoyant enough to be undisturbed by this strange question.

'It's a small town, Dr Armitage, don't ever forget that,' he said with a grating harshness that left her in no doubt as to his mood, and successfully ruined hers. 'Here's the supermarket!'

He reached across her and opened the door, thrusting it outwards with a suppressed fury, as if transferring all the antipathy he felt towards her into the action.

For a moment she sat there, as her mind battled to make sense of the man's behaviour. Then she shrugged her shoulders, and clambered out, turning to look at him as she stood in the open doorway.

'You're nuts!' she said succinctly, forgetting a training that should have provided a more scientific diagnosis. 'Nuts!' she repeated and slammed the door, to the delight and amusement of the Saturday morning shoppers.

CHAPTER FOUR

'I BET Steve's glad to have you here!' Dave Purvis, the surgeon, dropped the words into one of those pauses that occurred in all conversations, so that they echoed round the kitchen where most of the staff were polishing off a large meal after a particularly hectic day.

'You'd better ask him.' Jo looked across at Steve, challenging him to reply. Although she bitterly resented his attitude towards her, she would do or say nothing to give this close-knit community a suspicion that all was not well between them. What he chose to tell others was his business!

His eyes met hers, surprisingly soft yet puzzled, as if he found it hard to explain his reaction to her arrival. She heard him murmur something in reply, but the hum of general conversation drowned out the words.

She had seen little of him since the weekend. Brian's explanation that he had driven over to drop Karen's note on the veranda on Saturday morning had explained Steve's latest attack on her. Either he or a friendly gossip had missed Brian's arrival but had seen his departure only minutes later. What she could not understand was the strength of his reaction. He made no secret of the fact that he didn't like her. In fact, she remembered ruefully, just in case I hadn't got the message, he told me outright! So why is he concerned about my morals?

'Contact me if you've any problems at all,' the surgeon was saying, and Jo's mind returned to the present. 'I'll drop in early next week and check on

Josh; the others should be OK in your capable hands —
and don't forget, you're welcome at our place any
weekend that you can get away. Sometimes the only
way you'll have a proper break is to get out of town.'

He drained the last of his coffee, nudged his
anaesthetist who was flirting idly with Karen and
prepared to depart.

'Do come,' he added to Jo with a smile. 'My wife
loves visitors. Says it keeps her sane!'

'I'll try,' Jo assured him. 'See you next week.'

Her working day was far from over. She watched the
others depart, then returned to the wards, checking the
post-op patients who had left the recovery-room,
before going in to check on Josh.

Steve Hemming was there before her, standing by
the bed, looking down at the wizened little figure, pale
as a ghost, connected up to wires and tubes as he
battled back to consciousness.

'I think lymphoma is a better diagnosis than bowel
cancer,' she said quietly.

'I should have known! Should have guessed and
done a biopsy. It would have saved him the operation.'

'You say the most ridiculous things!' Jo whispered
angrily, shaking her head at such wilful self-condem-
nation. 'No one could have felt that lump, the way it
was hidden in there, and he would have had to have an
operation anyway, to move that section of the bowel
away from the mass before you could administer
chemotherapy.'

She glared at him, but he was lost in his own
thoughts. 'Dave's a good surgeon,' she continued, still
trying to pull him out of the depression that seemed to
have settled about him like a thick cloud. 'I'd say he's
given Josh a great chance to be treated successfully,
and then recover to lead a normal life.'

'I was dreading a huge tumour and a colostomy!' Steve spoke quietly, almost as if he was thinking aloud. 'He would have considered it such a terrible indignity, I hadn't dared mention it to him.'

He sank into the chair at the side of the bed, looking so drained and tired that Jo longed to comfort him.

'Well, there was no need to worry him about something that might never have happened,' she assured him philosophically, accepting that common-sense support was as much as he would accept from her. She nodded at the machine that was monitoring Josh's heartbeats and showing a strong, even pattern. 'He seems to have come through remarkably well for an eighty-year-old.'

'He's a tough old bugger,' Steve replied with genuine affection.

'You sound as if you know him well.'

'I've known him since I was twelve and first came to the west.'

Jo remained silent. There was a tantalising hint of sadness in his voice. Would he forget who she was and tell her more?

'My grandfather owned Cooraminya. My father had grown up there and hated the constant battle against an uncaring nature. The place is not big enough — not if you want to make a good living. He saw the way his parents had to work, simply to survive, saw their disappointment when floods swept all that work away or drought killed all the stock. He decided that he wasn't going to live the same way!'

'How could he escape it? Farms and properties pass from father to son and always have done. It was his legacy.'

'He ran away!' he told her simply. 'If you call it running away when you're twenty-five. Reckoned he'd done his bit to help his father, and went off to the city. His father was furious. They never spoke again!'

The strong, deep voice faded to a whisper, then gathered strength as if he needed the catharsis of speech.

'My father died soon after I was born. My mother remarried — to a doctor — and I didn't realise I had a grandfather until I was twelve.'

'What happened then?' She murmured the words, willing him to continue his reminiscing.

'My mother and stepfather decided I should know a bit about my heritage. It seems my mother had written to the old man when I was born, and again when my father died, but he hadn't replied. This time, she thought she'd make it impossible for him to ignore her.'

Jo watched his big body move restlessly in the chair, his long, strong fingers fiddling with the tubes that festooned the bed.

'She waited till the September holidays, put me on the bus, then rang the old fellow to say I was coming. Told him that she wanted nothing from him, but felt it was right that I should meet him.'

'And it was then that you met Josh.'

'Actually, Josh met me,' he told her, the severe lines in his face softening as his muscles relaxed into a reminiscent smile. 'My grandfather was a stubborn old man! He'd decided that I must be no good — brought up in the city by a doctor of all things!'

Isn't history repeating itself in the grandson? Jo wondered, hiding her wry delight that this man who had judged her so readily could not recognise the forerunner of his own behaviour! She held her peace.

'There was no way in the world he was going to meet any kid off a bus,' Steve continued. 'Fortunately, he'd mentioned Mum's phone call to Josh and he drove into town in an old jalopy he had and collected me. My first thought was that this was my grandfather. After those initial few days, I wished he were!'

'There was no great reconciliation scene, then?'

'No way! My grandfather had developed stubbornness to an art form! I stayed with Josh, and worked with him, while the old man ignored me.'

She felt a pang of sympathy for the little boy that he had been, the little boy that she still glimpsed occasionally with his rumpled hair and tired, vulnerable face.

'That must have been dreadful for you!'

'It could have been, but I found I loved the place. Loved the peace and quiet, the flat brown plains, and tired grey trees, the great arc of sky that seemed to stretch forever.' His eyes were hazed with the memory, lost in the wonder of that first discovery.

'Josh helped,' he continued quietly. 'He treated me like a man, and expected me to work as he worked— from dawn to dusk most days—but as we worked he told me things. Explained what we were doing in his slow, quiet voice, and the more I learned, the more I wanted to know.'

'So you went back?'

'Every holiday!' he said promptly. 'I still stayed with Josh, but the old man spoke to me from time to time, and, finally, I think, came to accept me. Not as a grandson, perhaps, but as an extra hand around the place.'

'Yet you always returned to the city, and you took up a career that could have kept you there.'

'It wasn't easy,' he sighed. 'I'd always wanted to be a doctor like my stepfather, but the bush now held a fascination for me that I couldn't resist. The old man tried to bribe me to stay—offering me the property if I gave up my "damn fool ideas about doctoring". It was

Josh who told me about my father's departure, who explained that Cooraminya was a good property, but not big enough to make the money you need to ride out the bad times.'

'I can understand why you're so concerned about him. He was probably more of a relative to you than your own grandfather.'

'He was indeed. Without Josh. . .' He paused for a long moment, and Jo sat silently, unwilling to break the spell between them that had softened this man's attitude towards her. 'It was Josh who suggested I combine medicine and the land. Josh who pointed out that people in the bush need doctors, too.'

'And your grandfather accepted you in the end and left the property to you?'

'No way! Not him! He left it to Josh, and I've bought it off him, after a great deal of arguing on his side and firm persuasion on mine. The silly old coot wanted to give it to me!' He smiled fondly at the still, frail figure on the bed. 'I had enough to give him a deposit that bought him his house in town, and he holds the mortgage on the rest, but I owe him more than money could ever repay.'

'You can repay a lot with love,' Jo said compassionately, seeing in his eyes the affection he had for the old man.

He looked across at her, his gaze holding hers and an arrested expression on his face, as if he was absorbing some extra meaning from her words. Then he shook his head and shrugged and she knew he was banishing the sentiment that had stirred his memory.

'Please call me if there's any change,' he said in his most professional voice, standing up and moving round the end of the bed. 'I'll be at the flat.'

* * *

'I'm telling this pretty doctor about Cooraminya,' Josh said to Steve, as he walked into the ward in the late afternoon a week later. The old man was recovering from the operation slowly, and Steve was reluctant to start the treatment until he was stronger.

'Telling us all for the one hundredth time,' another patient joked.

'Well, she doesn't know anything about the real west, poor lass, and no one else seems to be doing much to educate her.'

He frowned ferociously at Steve as he made his remark, and Jo felt that it was time she departed.

'When you're up and about I'll take you for a drive, and you can show me all these wonderful things,' she assured him. 'That's if your stories are true!'

'Might be weeks before I'm ready to go jolting about in a car,' he complained. 'You get this great hulking yobbo you call a doctor to show you round.'

'I have offered,' said the 'great hulking yobbo' with admirable restraint.

'Mustn't have asked right,' Josh told him disgustedly. 'Do it again so I can hear you—and make sure you remember the manners I taught you.'

Jo squirmed uncomfortably, and looked up at Steve apologetically.

'You don't have to,' she said quickly.

'I know that,' he replied, unfazed by the awkward situation the old man had contrived. He smiled at Josh, then around the ward at the other patients who were all propped on their pillows awaiting what was to come with transparent eagerness.

With one arm lifting to doff an imaginary cap, he bowed low, saying as he did so, 'Please, Dr Armitage, would you do me the great honour of accompanying me to Cooraminya on Sunday, so that you can see, with your own eyes, that all the stories this shameless old schemer is telling you must be taken with a grain of salt?'

There was a muttered expletive from Josh, and a burst of laughter and clapping from the rest of the audience. Jo could feel the heat burning in her cheeks, but knew she must respond. Catching one corner of her coat in her hand, she dropped a curtsy.

'I'd be delighted, sir,' she said, knowing that she was caught. She would have to go, because not only Josh, but the rest of the ward, would be anxiously awaiting her opinion of this, her first taste of what they all considered was the 'real west'.

'I'll see you later,' she said to Josh, as she moved past Steve towards the door. 'Much later, when I've worked out what the penalty is for bullying doctors.'

'Where's the fire?' Rosie asked as she burst through the door into the hallway.

'Oh, Rosie! Steve's asked me out to his property on Sunday.'

'What a good idea,' Rosie responded promptly. 'I don't know why I didn't think of it myself. It's time you saw a bit of the country.'

'Not you, too,' she groaned, heading for her office with Rosie trailing behind.

'Certainly. How will you ever know if you like the place or not, if you don't see anything of it?'

'I'm only here for another two months, you know,' she said, in a small voice. 'It doesn't matter whether I get to see much of the country or not.'

'We'll still need a doctor at the end of two months,' Rosie said. 'If you find you like the place, you might decide to apply for the permanent job.' She shut the door firmly and waved Jo towards her big chair, obviously determined to have this discussion now that the subject had arisen.

'The hospital board out here wants someone with more qualifications. All I've got are the O and G and anaesthetists' diplomas,' Jo told her.

'What they want and what they get are often two very different things. There was no one around earlier who was willing to take up the position, which is why you were appointed on a temporary basis. How do you know there'll be a more qualified person in another two months' time?'

'I still don't know if it's what I want,' Jo said quickly, covering a small surge of excitement that tingled through her veins.

'You must have thought about it to start the rural medicine training programme in the first place. What made you go back to Brisbane, and into research of all things? A blind man could see you're a "people" person.'

'There was a man in my life,' she explained with rueful honesty, accepting that the decision had been wrong for both of them. 'He wanted me in Brisbane, not traipsing around country hospitals.'

'Of course! Why is it always the women who are expected to give up their careers? What happened?'

'It's another story for another time, Rosie,' she said, unable to go into details of her infatuation with Martin or the disillusion and despair that had come out of it. She changed the subject. 'And how come you know so much about my past, anyway?'

'I checked,' Rosie told her, with a guilty smile robbing the words of offence. 'I like you, Jo, and we work well together—so much so that I decided to find out if I might possibly be able to persuade you to stay, and whether the board would accept you if I did.'

'Matron Strachan! Such conniving! I'm surprised at you!'

'Well?'

'Well what?'

'Would you stay if the board agreed?'

'I don't know, Rosie!' She shook her head sadly. 'I can't really say after just one month. I love the hospital, I love the work here, and the close contact with the patients. It's all I imagined rural medicine would be. . .'

'I can hear the "but" in your voice.'

'There are a few "buts" ——' including one very large one who is definitely on the board, she added silently as she shifted uncomfortably in the chair '—so let's wait and see.' She paused for a moment before adding, 'And Rosie?' The matron looked enquiringly at her. 'Thanks anyway! It's a great compliment to be asked. I sometimes feel very uncertain that what I'm doing is right. I seem to know so much less than all the rest of you. You've assured me no end.'

'What are friends for?' Rosie grinned at her. 'Come on; we'll check on the women's ward then go home. We've given enough time to the great god of medicine for one day!'

Rosie's words returned to Jo as she ate a belated dinner in front of the television. The movie she had started to watch had been interrupted by a call from the hospital, and she had lost the thread of the story to the extent that her mind kept wandering, round and round in frustrated circles, as she built up arguments for staying, then knocked them down again.

She did enjoy the work, she felt at home in the town, and found the patient contact most rewarding. The workload, shared now by two doctors, was not oner-ous, and there was plenty of variety to ensure one was never bored. Like the pins in a bowling alley, she stood up all the pros, but every time the one con came hurtling down through her mind and sent them all flying. Could she stay on when it meant working with Steve Hemming?

'Have you got that inhaler with you?' he asked as she walked across the back veranda to his car on Sunday morning.

'Good morning to you too,' she replied with a cheeky grin, determined not to let anything spoil the day. 'And yes, sir, I have my inhaler!'

He closed the passenger door then walked around and climbed in behind the wheel, but his own door remained open, and he did not start the engine. Instead he sat and looked at her, a puzzled frown furrowing his brow and the same perplexity she had noticed before deepening the blue of his eyes.

'I'm not an aggressive man,' he said in a mild voice, 'yet whenever we meet I get an urge to shake you, or smack you, or. . .'

'Or?'

'You wouldn't believe the "or",' he said, closing the door and turning on the ignition. 'I don't myself.'

They drove through town, and out along a road that ran north.

'I find it amazing how country towns just stop,' Jo said, as they sped along the dirt track through flat brown plains. A vague discomfort engendered by his unfinished sentence prompted her to speak. Any conversation was better than the awkward silence that had fallen between them. 'The streets end, the houses stop and beyond them there's nothing.'

'Even cities must end somewhere,' Steve replied, seemingly intrigued by her statement.

'I don't think so,' she said. 'I've been trying to work it out since I've been here. I think cities sort of fizzle out — so that their edges are blurred, not cut off sharply like these towns.'

'I sometimes think the comparison between life in the city and country is like that,' he said slowly. 'Out here, I seem to know my place in things, but in the city — other things intrude.'

'So you don't regret your decision to come out here?' Jo turned to look at him, studying his profile as if it might give her a clue to the inner workings of this man's mind or offer some clue as to what made him the way he was.

Why should I care? she wondered. She could not answer that, but knew that she did care. The thought irritated her, but then he answered.

'Only rarely,' he said in his deep, mellow voice, and again he stirred her curiosity.

When did he regret it? What were the rare moments when he questioned his decision? She looked away, out of the window, where tumbled balls of roly-poly chased each other across the bare earth. What does it matter? she thought. We're ships that pass in the night. Her eyes registered the barren, water-starved scene before her and she grinned at the simile. More like camels that pass in the desert, she amended.

'And what do you find to amuse you in this dry landscape?'

She turned to see his eyes flicking between her face and the road.

'Silly thoughts,' she explained briefly, then told him.

'Are we?' he asked, a depth in his voice that made it sound very serious, very sincere!

'Are we what?' She was playing for time, trying desperately to think of a reply.

'Are we simply ships that pass in the night?'

'Of course we are!' she said, thrusting aside a wave of denial that swept over her. 'I'm only here filling in, which is just as well as you don't even like me. You must be counting the days until I've gone! All we've got to do is work in comparative harmony until the time is up.'

He turned back to watch the road, and they travelled in silence again, until it strained between them. She had to talk!

'Tell me about Mary Jackson. Has she been diagnosed with Alzheimer's?' It was a reasonable guess. The vague, pretty, not yet old woman who roamed constantly through the wards and round the grounds had a file so short it was almost non-existent, and, apart from folic acid and Complex B tablets, needed no medication.

'Yes,' he told her, a deep sadness in his voice. 'She was only in her mid-forties at the onset, with three teenage kids. They shifted to the city because they thought treatment might be better there, but it accelerated the condition, so they came back here.'

'She's so young!'

He must have heard the pain in her voice, for he looked sharply at her, then continued. 'With early onset, the disease progresses rapidly. It's unlikely she'll live another year. We do what we can to keep her safe, and the family come whenever they can, but it's not much fun for them either.'

She shook her head, filled with the sense of defeat that incurable conditions always produced, and stared out of the window at the dusty landscape.

They came to a white-painted gateway, dusted with the red dirt from passing traffic. An old tin, nailed on a stump, served as a post-box, and painted on its rounded side was the fading name: 'Cooraminya'.

Here, low, scrabbly gums were scattered about the paddocks, and a straggle of sheep moved across the ground nibbling at tufts of dry Mitchell grass that only they could see. Ahead was the tall steel frame of a windmill, its sail still in the breathless air, and beneath its shadow she could see the low shape of a building that could be a house or sheds.

'I hope you're not expecting too much,' Steve said suddenly, as if it had just occurred to him that he was bringing a visitor to his home. 'Josh lived in a small cabin on the property, and the old man lived in the kitchen of the homestead. Since I took over there's been so much to do outside that I've left the house as it was.'

'Full of snakes?' she asked warily, a betraying tremor in her voice.

'Definitely not. The dogs live on the veranda and there's a cat that has adopted us. Between them they keep it free of unwelcome visitors.'

'Who looks after these animals if you live in town?'

'I've got a young fellow lives in the hut. He goes back home at weekends, but works around the place during the week.'

They pulled up in front of an unpainted, shabby but gracious homestead, set about three steps off the ground, with a wide veranda giving welcome shade. Three dogs rushed madly towards the car and were leaping and barking as they greeted their master.

'Back!' he roared as he came round to open the car door for her, and all three retreated to the veranda, where they stood, tongues lolling foolishly from their mouths, as they waited for their next order.

His hand reached up to take Jo's arm and steady her

as she jumped from the high seat to the ground.
Something in his touch burned through her like a
branding-iron. However, when he took his hand away
the skin felt cold and she shivered, foolishly looking to
see if his fingers had left a mark.

'I'll drop these stores in the kitchen then take you on
a tour of the place.' He lifted a coolbox and a card-
board carton out of the back as he spoke, and led the
way towards the house.

'Please don't bother to look after me. I'm sure you've
got plenty of work to do.'

'Always!' he said, turning back towards her with a
mock-groan, 'but I enjoy an excuse to neglect it and
spend a day remembering why I wanted this place so
badly.'

She looked up at him, surprised by the depth of
emotion in his voice.

'I'm looking forward to seeing it all,' she assured him
and followed him around the veranda to a screen door
that led into the kitchen.

It was a huge room, with an old wood-burning stove
dominating one end of it, and a long wooden table
stretching down the centre. At the end nearer the
stove, a plastic cloth marked off the section used for
eating, while a litter of papers in the middle indicated
it was also used as a desk. A clutter of odd bits of pipe
and machinery parts seemed to indicate a workbench,
and Jo smiled at the versatility. Work was not a
separate entity for farmers, but a part of their life,
permeating every minute of every day in some way.

While Steve unpacked his groceries, she continued
to study the room. Old wooden dressers, lining one
wall, held an array of blue and white china — probably
from his grandmother's trousseau, Jo guessed, walking
across to admire the pattern on the plates.

The cat had appeared and was rubbing itself around her ankles, a purring bundle of black fur, sleek and shining.

'Come on; I'll show you the rest of the house.' He jerked his head towards the door that led out at the far end of the room.

She followed him past the low divan that he must use as a bed when he stayed out here, up a step and into the house itself. It was only when she stepped on to the polished timber floors that Jo realised the kitchen had a different feel to it. She looked back. It was built on beaten earth, packed down tight, and shiny from the years of constant wear. It must have been the original building on the property, which explained its spaciousness and homely atmosphere.

The house was cool in spite of a temperature that was rising above the century. A wide passage ran through the building, dividing the formal dining-room and lounge on the right from the three bedrooms on the left. All the rooms opened through French doors on to the encircling veranda. In many ways it was just a typical old Queensland house, but there was something that set it apart.

'This furniture may be dusty, but it's beautiful,' Jo said in awe as she ran a finger over the dull surface of the dining-table. It was Victorian and she guessed mahogany, but it had a grace and beauty often lacking in some solid, heavy, more common Victorian pieces. The chairs were upholstered in a rich brocade in blue and green, and the same colour and pattern had been used on the long settee and high-backed chairs in the living-room. The material was faded but barely worn, and an impression that the house had never been used crept over Jo.

'My grandmother was Irish,' he said, as if in explanation of her thoughts. 'When she decided to settle out here, her family shipped out a houseful of furniture. Ask Josh about it some time. He tells how a wagonload of it arrived while the newly-weds were living in little more than a lean-to before the old man built what's now the kitchen. My grandfather wanted to sell it to buy stock, but my grandmother stood up to him and insisted on keeping it. Of course, it all had to be stored in town and it wasn't until after my father had left home that she finally got her house and saw her furniture set up inside it.'

Jo shook her head in wonder. Growing up in an age when function outshone beauty, and plastic had largely replaced timber, she had developed a passion for beautiful furniture and haunted antique shops in what spare time she had.

'If you like this, you'll love my next exhibit,' Steve said, smiling at her awe as she studied each piece in turn.

He led the way across the hall into the largest of the three bedrooms.

'It could be a room out of a museum,' she said, her eyes taking in the massive wardrobe and matching lowboy, the dressing-table with its winged mirrors and elegant chair, then the marble-topped wash-stand, complete with basin and jug in the same blue and white pattern she had already seen in the kitchen. 'It's a shame to see furniture like this neglected.'

Something about this bedroom was making her feel uncomfortable and she spoke more sharply than she had intended.

'I don't have enough time to do the work that's needed outside,' Steve said defensively, 'let alone start on polishing furniture. Even my cleaning lady refuses to polish it, although she comes out once a month to sweep the floors and flick the dust off.'

'That's one of the reasons you see so much painted and laminated furniture these days. People hate the extra work. They don't realise that it's worth the effort.'

Steve did not reply, but stood looking down at her as if searching for something in her face.

'That's true of more than furniture,' he said finally, and walked out of the room, leaving her trailing in his wake like a bit of flotsam thrown from an ocean liner.

'We'll walk down to the river,' he suggested when they came back out on to the front veranda. 'It's more a series of waterholes at the moment, but at least there's enough water for the sheep.'

The dogs fell in around them, roistering in front then dropping behind, glad to be with their master. The dry heat of the sun reflected back up from the hard-baked, red-brown earth, almost suffocating in its intensity. Jo felt it burning into her lungs although it was not yet midday. She was grateful when they reached the line of trees that marked the riverbank, but surprised by the steep banks that dropped away in front of them.

'Is there ever enough water in the river to reach up to the top of these banks?' she asked him as he scanned the riverbed for signs of anything amiss.

'Reach to the top and then flood,' he assured her. 'You get a bit of rain up north, the tail-end of a cyclone driving in from the Gulf, say, and this river will run a banker without any rain falling here.'

'Have you been here in a flood?'

'Once, when I was a kid. This is only the fourth year I've had the place but it's the sixth year of drought. The weather experts tell us it will break this wet season. They've had some rain round the Gulf, so it's possible they might be right.'

'You don't sound too convinced!'

'They have been known to be wrong,' he said, with heavy irony. 'Actually, I've got to believe them! If we don't get rain this season, what little water I've got will dry up and I'll lose the rest of the stock. It's no good thinking of agistment, because we're all in the same position.'

He shrugged and shook his head, accepting the hand that fate played in his life.

With her mind thinking through the implications of his words, and her eyes darting about as they assimilated the new surroundings, Jo followed him down a worn track towards the riverbed. There was a sharp, indefinable tang in the heavy air, and, as she brushed against the pendulous leaves of a pepper tree, she recognised the source. Pulling off some leaves, she crumbled them in her fingers, and sniffed at the bitter scent.

Steve led her along a sandy track, past tangled roots of she-oaks to where a stagnant pool of muddy yellow water lay. All around it, deep hoofprints showed the sheep could find their way down to it, and Jo felt a pang of sympathy for the poor animals who needed such unappetising liquid to survive.

'Oh, for heaven's sake!'

She turned at the oath, realising from his tone that he would probably have used far more expressive language if she had not been present. He was hurrying across to the far side of the dry river, and her eyes followed him, then fixed on the rusty red bundle that lay inert on the ground on the far side of the waterhole.

'I'll have to get the wagon and drag it away from the water,' he explained, as she reached his side and looked down at the huge red kangaroo that lay dead by the waterhole. 'Must have died this morning. In this heat you'd smell it ten miles away if it had been dead any longer. It'll pollute the water if I leave it here.'

'I see what you mean about always having plenty to do,' she said. 'Can I help? I'll get the car for you if you like.'

'Thanks, but I'll have to work out the best place to set it up, so I can use the winch to pull it up the bank.'

'Winch?'

'Most four-wheel drives round here have a winch fitted to the front. They can always get themselves out of trouble if necessary, and it comes in handy for little jobs like this.'

Jo found she was practically running to keep up with him, as he strode back towards the house. They climbed into the car and he drove it down a precipitous bank to the crossing then up the other side as easily as she drove her small car on the freeway. Parking it close to the top of the bank on the far side, directly above the carcass, he climbed out and waited while she came round to the front of the vehicle.

'See this switch here?' he said, pointing to a small electrical starter beside the coil of wire rope that she had not noticed before. 'When I yell "go" turn it on. I'll follow it up.'

He disappeared over the edge of the bank with the free end of the cable, and she peered down and watched as he hooked it around the dead animal. Within minutes the carcass was safely on the ground in front of the car, and Jo was feeling proud of the small part she had played in its removal.

'I haven't had any of these big fellows on the place lately. It's come in looking for water, and found it too late,' Steve explained as he detached the cable and rewound it on the winch. 'It means I'll have to do a

quick jaunt around the fences just to check he hasn't
broken one getting in. Hop in!'

'Do you drive around the fences?'

'No, that's too slow! I ride,' he said, adding with a
grin, 'On a dirt bike! We'll eat first then I'm afraid I'll
have to leave you for a few hours. Why don't you take
the wagon back to town and I'll come in on the bike
later?'

'I'll be quite happy to wait for you,' Jo assured him,
finding that she was relaxed and happy out here, away
from the hospital and its pressures. 'If a call comes, it's
better for you to have a proper vehicle. I can sleep, or
find something to read.'

'*Country Life* or farm machinery catalogues.'

'I'll be fine,' she assured him. 'If I get bored, I'll take
myself back to town!'

They pulled up outside the house once more, and
again she felt his eyes on her, studying her with a
puzzled intensity, as if she were some riddle he could
not solve.

CHAPTER FIVE

Jo SAW Steve depart with a feeling of suppressed relief. She hoped he had not realised how excited she was to be left in the house, to look again at the beautiful treasures that remained from a bygone time.

'Come on, cat,' she said. 'Let's see what we can find in these cupboards.'

She delved beneath the old-fashioned sink, pulling out old bottles with hardened remnants of their long-forgotten contents. She'd been right in assuming that Steve's grandfather — like his grandson — had simply used what they required and left the rest of the mystery bottles in their place.

Right at the back, she found what she was looking for — a wide-topped jar, thick with grimy dust, but with contents that turned a milky yellow when she shook it. Opening it gingerly, she sniffed, and then smiled. Her own grandmother had given her this recipe for furniture polish when she'd bought her first small antique tea-table, and there was no mistaking the pungent odour of boiled linseed oil, turpentine and vinegar.

Bearing her prize, and a piece of torn sheet off the divan in the kitchen, she made her way into the house. Common sense told her to start on a smaller piece, but she ached to see the dining-table come back to life, so set to work, humming to herself as she polished.

The room had darkened by the time she heard the bike return, but she had finished all but the last ornately turned and carved leg. She was sitting on the floor, rubbing furiously, when Steve called her name some time later.

'In here,' she said happily, still lost in the wonder of this glorious piece of furniture.

'What have you been doing?' he demanded as she emerged from under the table.

'Turn on some lights and you'll see,' she said, excited by her efforts and wondering what effect the results might have on him.

'There are no lights in here,' he told her. 'The generator provided power to the kitchen, but my grandmother died soon after the house was finished, so when the power came through the old man never bothered to have it connected to the main house.'

'But there are fittings,' she said, amazed by his story — and by a house where lights did not switch on and off at the press of a button.

'It's all wired,' he explained; 'it's just not connected.'

The darkness in the room was deepening as the sun sank across the dusty plains and took its light with it. Jo felt a bitter disappointment. It was because she was tired, she knew, working so hard in this dreadful heat, but she'd wanted him to see the table, to experience the soft, rich patina of the wood and share the magic of its gleaming beauty.

As if sensing her feelings he reached out to touch her on the arm.

'Wait right here,' he said, and disappeared in his silent way back towards the kitchen.

I'm too tired to move away, she thought, and stood where she was, letting the peace seep into her bones.

She saw the light before she heard him coming, and when he placed the old kerosene lamp on the table she drew in her breath with an audible gasp.

'That's better than electricity, isn't it?' he said softly, walking around the table.

The timber shone with a rich red glow, and the flame was reflected so that it seemed to flicker in its depths.

'It's mahogany,' she said, rubbing her hand over the smooth shining surface. 'It's really a golden timber, but the Victorians polished it to look red. That's why you get those golden depths in it.'

'Thank you, Jo,' he said very quietly, reaching out to take her chin and turn her face up to his.

She looked up, trying desperately to read his thoughts, wondering if he was also caught in the fine web of confusion that held her in thrall. His eyes were hidden from her behind those hooded lids, but his face seemed soft and gentle in the flickering lamplight, as gentle as the kiss that he bent and left, with infinite tenderness, on her parted, wondering lips.

His lips were cool, and his skin smelt fresh and clean. He'd showered and changed into clean clothes before coming to find her!

He lifted his head, only inches, and she felt his warm breath brush across her skin, as temptingly erotic as the kiss itself. Mesmerised by some potent spell he had cast about her, she remained motionless, her face still lifted to his, waiting. . .

He bent again, as she had known he would, but this time the lips that met hers were fierce and demanding, pressing against her soft skin with an urgency that revived her tired body and fired her soul with a wordless longing. His hands moved to hold her shoulders, his grip firm yet tender, as if he feared that she might break if he unleashed the full strength of his long fingers against her fragile bones. With a deliberate control, he held her away from him, although her body longed to melt against his, to fit itself to his contours, and find ease in his strength.

She felt his lips move, parting hers still more, and his tongue, moist and hard, probed her mouth, teasing at the soft skin, and darting in and out as she gasped for air and fought to control the tumult he was arousing with a single kiss.

Was it a minute or an hour later that he raised his head and dropped his hands, stepping away from her as if putting distance between himself and some unfamiliar object?

'Of course, it's sheer stupidity to undertake that sort of work in the heat of a summer's day.' The cool, emotionless tone of his voice as well as the judgemental words broke the spell, and Jo shivered. He took the dirty cloth out of her nerveless fingers and wiped away the sweat that beaded her forehead. Her body responded again to his touch, a warmth like fever spreading through it. She was suddenly, embarrassingly, aware of her appearance. She could feel her hair, clinging in damp strands to her forehead, and see the dirt that grimed her hands. Her face was probably just as bad!

'I'll take you back home for a shower, then we'll see what the hospital kitchen is offering for dinner. Does that sound like a nice, romantic evening to round off the weekend?'

Romantic? Her mind whirled. He had kissed her, but what was a kiss these days? Was he flirting with her? Would that kiss lead to something later, some words of interest in her, some suggestion that he might like her in spite of his preconceived ideas? Hiding her confusion, she answered him, forcing herself to be as matter-of-fact as he had been.

'I can't think past the shower at the moment. I'm sure food will appeal once I'm clean.'

She was pleased at the even tone of her voice, in spite of the heat that still simmered in her body. I can be just as blasé as you, Dr Hemming, she told him silently, following him out to the kitchen where he blew out the lamp and replaced it on the top shelf of the cupboard before chasing the cat outside and leading her towards the car.

As he drove back towards town, she asked him about the fences and sat contentedly, happy to listen to his deep voice explaining the damage he had found and the problems kangaroos could cause. Her inner turmoil settled as she let his words flow over her.

'I'll do a round and check on what's been happening, then join you in the kitchen in about an hour. Suit you?' he added with a casual sidelong glance.

'Sounds fine,' she said, as the car swung into the hospital drive and round the back to her house. 'If there's been any great drama someone would have phoned us, wouldn't they?'

Earlier in the day, she had noticed the small mobile phone clipped to his belt.

'Most probably,' he agreed. 'The miracles of modern communication mean that doctors never get a day off!'

'Now that I'm here, you could always leave it at home when you're not on call.' She regretted the words as soon as they were out of her mouth. Would it break the tenuous harmony that seemed to exist between them at the moment? Remind him who she was, and rekindle his dislike?

'I suppose I could,' he said cheerfully, as she opened the door and jumped out. 'Meanwhile, I am on call, and had better show my face over there. I'll see you soon.'

He smiled again — a warm, conspiratorial smile that made Jo's skin tingle. She headed for the bathroom.

'Oh, for heaven's sake,' she muttered, using what had become the hospital catchphrase as she saw her face in the mirror. 'No wonder the man was smiling. I should be grateful he wasn't laughing his head off.'

Her face was streaked with dirt where she had rubbed her hands across the dust that had settled as she worked, and dirty tracks led down across her face where beads of perspiration had slid through the grime. Suddenly she felt tired, and stupid tears of self-pity welled up in her eyes.

'Drat that man,' she said aloud as she turned from the mirror, and pulled off her dirty clothes. 'Why should I care what I look like when I'm with him?'

'Surely this isn't the grotty little specimen I brought home earlier?' he asked with a wide grin when she appeared in the kitchen some time later. He was getting cutlery out of the drawer and proceeded to set the table as he spoke.

Jo felt a blush stealing into her cheeks. She was aware that she had made a special effort as she dressed, although, all the while, her instincts were shouting, Don't do it! Don't go to any trouble for this man who dislikes you so much. Don't read too much into one kiss!

'I was a mess, wasn't I?' she admitted ruefully.

'A thoroughly delightful mess,' he responded. 'I should be taking you out somewhere fancy to show my gratitude for all the work you did, but there's nowhere fancy to go in Warilla on a Sunday night.'

Again an unaccustomed heat crept into Jo's cheeks and she hastened to move the conversation back on to a less personal level.

'I love old furniture,' she explained, pulling out a chair and sinking into it. 'If you don't object, I'd be happy to spend some of my free time restoring it.'

'You can't possibly mean it,' he said, opening the oven to see what was waiting for them.

'Of course I do! I'd love to see it all polished, the way it should be. Even if no one does it again for years, it will be good for the furniture as well.'

'Then feel free,' he told her, plainly puzzled by her interest. 'You saw where the key was kept. Just make sure you let someone know when you're going and when you'll be back, in case of an accident.' He looked at her in silence for a moment, then added, 'And Jo?'

'Yes?'

'Thank you,' he said, transporting her, with the simple repetition of two common words, back into that lamplit room, her memories of his kiss burning through her once more.

She fiddled with her cutlery, concentrating on setting the knife and fork exactly parallel, as if it were of tremendous importance to have them just right.

'Roast,' he announced, switching again from poetic to prosaic, and confusing her even more.

Melly was off duty, but her assistant had left a large platter of roast lamb and baked vegetables. Jo forgot her contradictory reactions to her colleague as soon as Steve lifted it out of the oven and set it on the table between them. Whatever else was wrong with her, her appetite was not affected. They discussed the hospital as they ate, unaware that the gods were on their side for once, allowing them to finish their meal uninterrupted.

'Thank goodness you're still here! Could one of you come right away?' Karen rushed into the kitchen and stood facing them, her hands clasping each other so tightly that her knuckles showed white.

'Janey Lamb came in about half an hour ago, with bad, cramping sort of pains in her abdomen,' she explained as they both followed her out, their empty plates abandoned as they faced what might be an emergency. 'She's had her appendix out, but says it feels different from the pain she had then.'

'How long's she been having them?' It was Steve who put the obvious question to the senior sister.

'They started after lunch, so she lay down. Her period is late and she thought they might be menstrual cramps, but they got steadily worse. Bill was out at his parents' place, and when he got home she looked so sick he brought her straight here.'

'How was she when you admitted her?' Steve asked as they paused outside the door to Casualty, preferring to hear as much as they could from Karen before seeing the distressed woman.

'Her pulse was high—a hundred and twenty—and her blood-pressure low, but not lower than some people are normally. Since then the pressure's dropped and her pulse has become thready.'

Steve led them through, and Jo saw the young woman, panting on the high trolley, her body twisting in pain, and her breath coming in heavy gasps.

'Take some blood grouping, Sister, and set up an IV. If we need blood and can't match it, we'll use plasma.'

He bent over Janey, murmuring to her as he felt her distended abdomen, his hands moving with a practised sureness that made Jo feel momentarily envious.

'It's possibly an ectopic pregnancy. We'll operate straight away and just hope it hasn't ruptured, although I don't like the signs.'

He looked across at Jo, and it struck her that he was the complete professional, as sure with this woman's life in his hands as he was with the winch cable out on his property.

'Bill, her husband, is outside. If she's been in pain it's unlikely she's eaten, but check with him, and tell him what we suspect and what we're going to do.'

He turned his attention back to Janey as Jo left the room and she heard him speaking quietly and soothingly as he questioned her about known allergies and explained what he thought had happened.

'I'm Jo Armitage,' she said quietly to the worried young man — scarcely more than a teenager — who paced restlessly up and down the wide hallway. 'Dr Hemming is with your wife. He thinks it's what we call an ectopic pregnancy. It's important that we operate immediately.'

She glanced at him, seeing the colour fade beneath the freckled skin. Almost before her eyes, the face matured and she saw a shadow of the man he would eventually become.

'Could you explain it to me?' he asked. 'First, what's wrong and then what you're going to do.'

'Of course,' she agreed, reaching over on to the front desk to grab a pencil and piece of paper. 'Sit over here; it's easier to draw it.'

Knowing that she would be needed in Theatre any moment, she drew hastily, showing him the fallopian tubes that took ova from the ovary to the uterus.

'It just sometimes happens that a fertilised egg can lodge in one of the tubes by mistake. We don't know why it happens, but we do know that it probably happens more often than we think. Quite often the body sorts it out naturally, but occasionally, as in Janey's case, it continues to grow there. The pain she's feeling is because it has grown big enough to be aggravating the tube. When this happens, the tube can rupture, and there is a risk of peritonitis, and internal haemorrhaging.'

'That might have happened already,' he said, and Jo heard the panic rising again in his voice.

'That's what we're afraid of, and why we're operating immediately. Even if the tube has ruptured, we can clear it all up quite quickly. I've got to go now. I'll have to do the anaesthetic for Dr Hemming. We shouldn't be too long, and Janey will certainly feel much better by the time we're finished, even with an operation to get over.'

'I can wait here?'

'You certainly can! She'll want to see you as soon as she wakes up. One of the nurses will get you tea or coffee as soon as we're organised in Theatre.'

'Thanks, Dr Armitage,' he said, in the polite tones of a schoolboy.

'Save the thanks till later,' she said as she departed, hoping that her words would be prophetic and that Janey's case would be as simple as she had made it sound. As always in these situations, her mind considered what they would have to do, and she fought down a queasy feeling as she realised what a ruptured tube could mean.

They were waiting for her when she reached the theatre. Rosie had arrived to assist Steve, and Janey was prepped and already asleep from the Diprovan Steve would have administered as pre-med.

'Bill OK?' Steve greeted her, and she nodded, checking out the equipment and selecting the drugs she would need from the cabinet.

'He's worried but understands what we've got to do.

How long do you think you'll need?' she asked him, as she measured out the drugs.

'With luck, an hour, but if it's ruptured. . .' Steve's voice tailed away as they all contemplated the possibilities. Infection could spread so quickly, and, even with modern antibiotics, the mortality-rate from septicaemia was still high.

'She's young and healthy,' Jo reassured him as she dripped the Ethrane into the machine. Her eyes were fixed on the screen of the monitor as she watched for any adverse reaction to the anaesthetic she had chosen. Knowing that it suited most people was reassuring, but every case was different and no one knew when that one person in a thousand would come up.

'Did you consider surgery as a speciality?' she asked as she watched Steve work with a speed and efficiency she had to admire.

'Fleetingly,' he said, his eyes on his fingers as he opened up the transverse incision he had made low on the abdomen, and clamped off tiny blood vessels, before reaching into the tube.

'The call of the bush was too strong?' she teased.

'The call of Josh Evans, more like,' snorted Rosie. 'He'd decided Steve would be Warilla's new doctor before the poor boy was halfway through his degree.'

'I've no regrets,' Steve said, and Jo remembered what he had said earlier and knew that the 'no regrets' was not entirely true.

'None?'

Rosie was also probing this rash statement. She knew him well, and probably knew exactly what he was not revealing.

'Only that we never get any of the nice surgical procedures,' Steve complained, as he examined the swollen ball of tube. 'Since they invented flying surgeons all we ever get are the emergencies like Janey here, and accident victims that we patch up so someone else can perform the miracles.'

He fell silent, turning the pinkish mass very carefully in his hands.

'Could you look at this?' He raised his eyes to Jo as he spoke and again she felt a jolting shock of recognition. She left her place and moved to his side, alerted by the excitement in his voice.

'There's no sign of a rupture,' she said quietly.

'No, and look where it is! I think we could express it through the fimbrial end of the tube, and save the tube itself.'

'But wouldn't even the existing damage to the tube predispose Janey to another ectopic on this side? Providing there's no problem with her ovary on the other side, she's still got a very good chance of having children.'

'Rosie?'

'I think I agree with Jo. I know all about trying more conservative treatments in surgery, but if adhesions or scar tissue in that tube is likely to mean this will happen again, then she's better taking her chances with one ovary and tube in good working order.'

Steve looked from one to the other. 'Would we do it differently if we were in the city?' he asked, his voice tight with doubt. 'That's the thing that always worries me!' His frustration was clearly visible in his eyes. 'Am I giving these people less than first-class service because we're so isolated?' He was examining the other ovary and tube as he spoke, ensuring there were no signs of abnormality.

'Just because the decisions you make might be different,' Jo said, thinking through what he had said, 'it doesn't mean they're second-class. The lives of your patients are different, and so are their needs. GPs in the city can prescribe something for a patient, then monitor the reaction by seeing them daily or weekly, whatever the need. It may be a marginally better treatment than you prescribe to a patient who lives on a property two hours out of town, but you know it will work for him and give him the freedom he needs to follow his normal lifestyle.'

'The tube has gone,' Steve said. 'I bow to your combined feminine wisdom. I was probably only thinking of myself, because I was presented with an opportunity to show off my surgical skills!'

'Well, at least you admit it,' Rosie told him forthrightly. 'When I think of some of the things people do to boost their own egos—and I mean people in all walks of life, not just doctors—I get so angry!'

'And an angry Rosie is not something to take lightly,' Steve said flippantly as he sutured the wound and stood aside for Rosie to dress it.

'I'm so glad it wasn't worse,' Jo said, checking the monitor and noting with satisfaction that Janey's blood-pressure and respiration were good and her pulse still high but regular.

'You're officially off duty, Jo; we'll clean up here,' Rosie said, as they readied Janey for her transfer to the small post-op room before being settled into a ward.

'And you're not?' Jo asked, knowing that Rosie worked far more hours than she was supposed to, especially when emergencies arose. 'I'll let you clean up the mess you've both made in here, but I'll see Bill again and explain what's happened, then wait with Janey till she wakes. She might need a bit of reassuring.'

'That division of labour lets me out. It looks as if I

can go home to bed,' Steve said smugly, and Jo felt a tremor of disappointment.

The kiss meant nothing, she told herself again. It was a thank-you for polishing his old table, that's all! For a girl who doesn't want entanglements, you're not behaving too sensibly.

She was putting away the unused drugs in the cabinet in the ante-room, which was more an alcove off the theatre. She listened to the banter between Steve and Rosie with half an ear while her own thoughts chased each other through her mind.

'You just feel left out!' Rosie was saying to him. 'You can't get used to the fact that it's not *your* hospital any more!'

'There've been other superintendents here in my time,' Steve argued, 'and I've survived.'

'Only because you've been away or busy studying! There was only one relief superintendent that you ever trusted to look after your hospital, and that was Hilary.'

'Well,' Steve admitted readily enough, 'Hilary was different!'

'Very,' said Rosie with a cryptic emphasis that Jo could not understand, but she lingered on unncessarily, hating her own unreasonable curiosity but unable to stop herself from wanting to hear more about the woman that they had all thought Steve would marry.

'How is she, by the way?' Rosie asked.

'Fine,' was the prompt reply. 'You'll see for yourself how fine shortly—she's coming up for a quick holiday next week.'

'I'll be off, then,' Jo said, locking the cabinet and turning to walk out of the door. She masked the irrational disappointment Steve's words had caused with a false cheerfulness, but knew she must escape before the stupid tears that had filled her eyes betrayed her.

'Bring her over to dinner one night,' Rosie was saying, as Jo left the room, her mind seething with the implications of those last few scraps of conversation.

Bill was hovering outside the door, his face white with tension. Immediately, she put aside her personal chagrin and set herself to reassure him.

'The operation went beautifully and Janey will be awake again very soon,' she said quickly, anxious to allay his fears. 'I'm going in to check her now and will let you see her as soon as she comes out of the anaesthetic. She'll still be dopey and will need more sleep, but I'm sure that a few minutes with you will only help her recovery.'

'Had it ruptured?'

'No, but we had to tie off that tube. Everything else looks fine, so you'll still be able to have children. I'll talk to Janey about that as she gets better, but in the meantime she's more likely to believe you than me, so do reassure her if she's anxious.'

'Thanks, Dr Armitage. I must say it's great having a woman doctor out here for a change, especially for the girls!'

Jo grinned. His simple compliment had cheered her up no end, and pushed her own, less rewarding thoughts to the back of her mind.

'Thank you, too!' she said, with sincere gratitude. 'Now, I'll go and check her. We'll bring her back through here to the ward, so if you wait just a little longer you can go back with her.'

'When are you going to operate?' Janey was asking the nurse as Jo entered Post-op.

'It's all over,' Jo reassured her, pleased that the modern anaesthetics left so little residual effects on patients that they were totally unaware they had been asleep. 'You'll be a bit sore for a few days but we'll give you analgesics for the pain, and have you out of here in no time at all!'

She stood beside the trolley, and checked Janey with professional efficiency. Certain that all was well, she detached the wires that led to the monitor.

'We'll leave the drip in until tomorrow,' she told the nurse on duty. 'She should be able to take fluids by then. Can you push the stand and I'll wheel her back to the ward? Matron is still around; she'll want to see her settled in bed before she leaves for the night.'

'Where's Bill?' Janey asked as they prepared to move her again.

'Waiting to see you just outside the door,' Jo told her with a smile.

As they pushed through the swing doors, Bill's anxious face appeared, his red hair standing up on end where he had ruffled it with restless hands.

'You OK, love?' he asked, his young man's voice cracking as he spoke. The tender desperation with which he grasped her hand, and the shining love in his eyes as he looked anxiously down at his wife, said more than any words. Jo found herself turning away, tears once more prickling at her eyelids.

FREE! THIS CUDDLY TEDDY BEAR!

You'll love this little teddy bear. He's soft and cuddly with an adorable expression that's sure to make you smile.

PLAY THE MILLS & BOON
LUCKY
STARS
GAME!

Scratch away the silver panel. Then look for the matching star sign to see how many gifts you're entitled to!

 WORTH 4 FREE BOOKS, A FREE CUDDLY TEDDY AND FREE MYSTERY GIFT.

 WORTH 4 FREE BOOKS, AND A FREE CUDDLY TEDDY.

 WORTH 4 FREE BOOKS.

 WORTH 2 FREE BOOKS.

YES! Please send me all the free books and gifts to which I am entitled. Please also reserve a Reader Service subscription for me. If I decide to subscribe I shall receive six superb new titles every month for just £11.40 postage and packing free. If I decide not to subscribe I shall contact you within 10 days. The free books and gifts will be mine to keep in any case. I understand that I am under no obligation whatsoever. I may cancel or suspend my subscription at any time simply by contacting you. *I am over 18 years of age.*

6A4R

MS/MRS/MISS/MR _____

ADDRESS _____

_____

_____

POSTCODE _____ SIGNATURE _____

◄ TEAR OFF AND POST THIS CARD TODAY! ◄

Mills & Boon Reader Service
FREEPOST
P.O. Box 236
Croydon
Surrey
CR9 9EL

NO
STAMP
NEEDED

CHAPTER SIX

'CAN I go home today?'

Janey's bright face crumpled doubtfully as Jo walked into the ward. All the patients in a hospital this size became friends, but an extra bond had developed between herself and this young woman. If doctors were allowed to have favourites, she would have to say that Janey and old Josh would be at the top of her list.

'As long as you don't overdo things once you get there,' she chided. 'I'd rather you didn't go back to work for another week. Sitting in a solicitor's office all day mightn't be hard physically, but any type of work imposes a strain on the body. Short walks for exercise, and some flopping around in the pool once your wound is healed, and you'll be as good as new in no time.'

'Not quite!'

Jo looked at her sombre face. 'Janey,' she pleaded. 'We've been all through this. You're young and healthy and you have every chance of having children. If you even suspect you might be pregnant, go straight to Dr Hemming, or come to me here, and we'll test you and check, right from the beginning.'

'But what if it does happen again?'

Jo sighed and busied herself with a very thorough examination while she wondered what to say next! She had explained to both of them about the tests that could verify that the foetus was in the uterus, and about the use of laparoscopy if they were still in doubt, but she could not dispel the lingering uneasiness from

Janey's mind, as she fought her disappointment as well as a sense of inadequacy.

'Now listen, young lady,' she said, looking up from the hieroglyphics on Janey's chart. 'Bill married you for yourself, and, while the thought of having a mother for his children may have featured somewhere in his thinking, I doubt very much that it was his prime motivation.' She was rewarded by a shy, reminiscent grin, and continued, 'There are plenty of women who find out after marriage that they're infertile — or that their husbands are! It doesn't destroy the marriage. In many cases it strengthens it, as, together, they decide what they'll do about it.'

'We've talked about adopting,' Janey told her.

'That's good, because, although the chances are it won't be necessary, it shows you're taking a practical approach to things. In the meantime, go home, rest, and, above all, don't worry.'

'"What will be will be", you reckon?'

'Exactly!' Jo smiled down at the pretty young woman.

'Can I come and see you if I'm worried again?'

'Any time! But right now give Bill a call and tell him he can come and get you, then have a shower and put on that beautiful dress he brought in the other day, so you'll be ready when he comes.'

Jo left the ward with a nagging feeling of dissatisfaction, and tried to pin it down. False modesty aside, she knew that she was performing well at work; knew she was handling the variety of tasks with ease and enjoyment and facing the various crises that punctuated each week both calmly and competently.

'Problems?'

Steve's tall frame blocked the light that usually

streamed through the glass doors at the front of the building.

'Why do you ask?' she said sharply, realising that a woman she had not seen before had come in with him and was hovering behind his shoulder.

'Could it be because you're standing in the middle of the foyer, frowning ferociously enough to frighten off any patient who might be misguided enough to wander in?' he responded promptly, a teasing lilt that she had not heard before lightening his remark.

She shook her head, unable to reply, then smiled at the woman who had emerged from behind him.

'Janey OK?' he persisted, and she frowned again.

'She's fine! Going home today!'

'Great!' He shrugged his bulky shoulders, then added, 'Well, if you're not going to share your burden, I'd better introduce you to Hilary. She did a temporary stint here a few years back and can't stay away from the place.'

I bet she can't, Jo thought cattily, pasting a false smile across facial muscles that had suddenly grown stiff.

'I'm Jo Armitage,' she said, holding out her hand politely.

'Hilary Waring.'

As they shook hands, Jo's quick eyes flicked over the tall, blonde woman, recognising the fine bone-structure that gave her a lean elegance even in old baggy shorts and a loose singlet top.

'Do you mind my coming?' Hilary asked, her deep voice as cool and pleasing as her appearance. 'I do love to catch up with all the staff, and even see the patients that I might remember.'

'Feel free,' Jo told her, wishing she could infuse a little more warmth into her voice. 'I know everyone's been looking forward to your visit.' Everyone but me, she added silently. 'I'll be in the office.'

She dashed away, more disturbed than ever now, as she puzzled over the irrational irritation Hilary's visit had produced.

'Problems?' Rosie was slumped in the visitor's chair in her office and unconsciously echoed Steve's question.

'Not really,' she responded, feeling the cloud of inexplicable gloom descending rapidly. 'Janey's going home this morning.'

'She'll be fine,' Rosie reassured her.

'So I keep telling her!' She sighed.

'Then what's upsetting our little ray of sunshine today? This isn't like you, Jo.'

Sinking into the huge chair, she sighed again. 'It's Janey going home,' she said slowly, as she struggled to clear her thoughts by putting them into words. 'I suppose it's made me realise that I won't be here to see what happens to her and Bill. I won't know if she gets pregnant again, and has kids. And what about Josh? We're waiting until he's over the operation before starting chemo, so he'll only have had one, or at the most two treatments before I have to go! I've never had this close a relationship with patients before and——'

'You don't have to go,' Rosie interrupted vehemently. 'You've fitted in here so well, Jo. Apply for the permanent position and stay on in Warilla,' she pleaded.

'No doubt you try to persuade all your locums to do the same,' Jo mumbled, unswayed by the appeal as she thought of Hilary.

'Never been able to,' Rosie told her succinctly. 'The only time we've had locums was when Steve was superintendent and away for a course. It was always understood he would be back to take over the job.'

'And since he resigned, you've had no one?' The thought appalled Jo, diverting her mind from her own problems as she realised again the stress it must have placed on Steve, as the only doctor in town.

'One person who was appointed before you. He stayed two weeks and left for overseas, unable to face the reality of rural life or the pattern of the work here.'

'Boring one day, frantic the next!'

'Warilla boring?' Rosie teased, smiling as if she realised that Jo had thrown off her shadow of depression.

'Who says Warilla's boring?' Steve's head had appeared round the door, and Jo shuddered as she realised what his reaction would be to Rosie's reply. As soon try to stop a runaway train as halt this conversation, she thought resignedly, as Rosie said brightly,

'Jo!' and pointed her finger towards the culprit as if to emphasise the point.

Watching him closely, Jo saw his brows draw together in a quick frown of distaste, but there was a quick flicker of something else in his eyes. It looked like disappointment!

'It depends on the work you want to do,' came the cool voice Jo had heard earlier. She did not need Rosie's delighted cry of 'Hilary!' to tell her who was coming.

As if suddenly remembering where she was, Rosie ushered Hilary out of Jo's office, chattering excitedly to her as she went. It left Jo with a feeling of exclusion, as if she was on the outside, looking in at a scene of happy camaraderie. The glance she threw at Steve, still hovering in the doorway, was one of total dissatisfaction as her earlier depression returned.

'Would you mind if I went to Cooraminya this afternoon and took out my bad temper on your furniture?'

'If that's how you feel,' he agreed, shrugging casually, although his blue eyes still searched her face. 'Perhaps you'd like to come over for dinner when you get back to town. Eight o'clock?'

She was nonplussed! There had been no personal conversation between them since their visit to the property last Sunday, and she had assumed that, having fulfilled his promise to Josh, he would continue to ignore her socially.

'Hilary will enjoy your company,' he added, reminding her of his guest and dashing the tiny spark of excitement that had leapt, unbidden, in her heart.

She pushed aside one of the piles of papers that littered her desk, and pulled another equally depressing pile towards her, hoping he would get her message.

'I'll see you tonight, then,' she said, dropping her eyes to the papers in what she hoped would be an unmistakable gesture of dismissal.

She had enjoyed the solitude of the afternoon at Cooraminya. The house seemed to weave a magic about her, as if wrapping her protectively in the secrets of its past, and the beautiful furniture repaid her efforts, gleaming richly in the dim rooms like forgotten treasures in an old junk yard.

Pleasantly tired by the time she returned home, she showered and dressed reluctantly. She did not want to go to Steve's place for dinner, she decided, as she changed from a light linen shift—the vivid pink was too shocking—into her flowered silk—no, too formal—and, ultimately into loose-fitting silk trousers and a sleeveless waistcoat top, both an unobtrusive deep cream in colour!

Such uncharacteristic indecision nagged at her mind, but she thrust it aside. I need a special compartment in my mind for unwanted thought, she told her reflection, as she clipped on a pair of glittery gold earrings, and hung the matching chain around her neck, where it lay, gleaming brightly, against her tanned skin.

She had driven past the converted house many times, and wondered about the place that Steve had made his home. From outside, it was a neat, weatherboard cottage, entirely lacking in character, the only distinguishing feature being a rather dull brass plate fixed to the front fence.

On entering, in response to his, 'Come in,' she found the inside equally uninspiring. The only touch of colour was Hilary, clad in a flowing scarlet and gold caftan that added a hint of the exotic to the purely functional room.

The two women nodded politely at each other while Steve made hostly noises about drinks. Despite the austere surroundings, he looked at ease, and Jo felt that he was more relaxed than she had ever seen him, his bulky body moving with an easy grace in the small room, as he poured fizzing liquid into a glass. Was it Hilary's presence? she wondered, then quelled the nasty spurt of resentment the thought caused. Maybe he was always this relaxed at home, she decided, imagining the long, loose limbs stretched out on the couch.

'Tell me what happended between you and Martin Collins.'

The politeness in Hilary's voice didn't detract from the command! Jo had barely raised the glass of icy squash to her lips when the words were fired at her. All other wayward images flew out of her mind. As she sat, frozen by the thought of having to discuss Martin with these relative strangers, she heard Steve's voice.

'Hilary doesn't believe in beating around the bush,' he told her, with an apologetic wink.

No doubt he's remembering my reaction when he raised Martin's name once before, she thought wryly, sipping at her drink while she fought to regather her composure.

'We met, we got engaged, we got unengaged,' she said unemotionally. 'In between all that excitement, there were the normal things that happen in relationships.'

She was determined to say no more. Martin hadn't killed himself for love, as Steve assumed. She felt no guilt about that, but had her questions prompted further, quiet investigations? Had those investigations pushed him to that final resolution? These doubts, nagging at her conscience, had prompted her to accept this position, but there was no escape!

'I don't mean that.' Hilary waved a hand impatiently. 'I can imagine any woman falling in love with Martin.' She paused, then added reminiscently, 'I was more than half in love with him myself at one stage!'

'You were?' Jo queried lightly, glad to shift the focus of the conversation. Somehow, the idea of Martin with this cool, sophisticated beauty was quite acceptable.

Hilary smiled, a secret, reminiscent smile that made Jo wonder exactly what had been the relationship between them.

'Yes,' she said at last. 'I was quite carried away, wasn't I, Steve?' She turned to their host for confirmation, her lovely lips curling upwards in a warm, conspiratorial smile that made Jo wince. 'Until I realised that Martin was totally selfish, totally absorbed with himself, with what he was doing, and what he wanted to do. He was obsessed by Martin to the exclusion of all else, and, providing his needs were met, then any woman in his life could simply make her own arrangements.'

'That's a strong judgement coming from you, Hilary,' Steve protested.

Jo remained silent, caught up in the unmistakable truth of Hilary's character-reading. She agreed, but was surprised she had never analysed their relationship herself. The humiliation of Martin's rejection, even though, by then, she no longer loved him, had scarred her. His scathing condemnation of her 'righteous attitude' and, later, his derisive remarks about her lack of sensuality, had been too potent for common sense to intervene. She had simply accepted his reading of her character and, like a wounded animal, crawled away to attempt to rebuild her shattered self-esteem.

'I was really wondering why you left the research project,' Hilary explained, bringing the conversation back to where she wanted it with a sure touch.

'I wanted to work with people again,' Jo answered, hoping they would not hear the evasion in her voice. She looked around the room as she answered, desperately seeking something she could use to divert the conversation. Hilary sat alongside her on the three-seater leather settee, while Steve lounged against a tall bookcase.

'Research too boring for you?' he asked, his voice a fine example of polite indifference, but Jo sensed the hidden gibe and squirmed.

'Boring? But you left your place on the rural medicine programme to join the research team,' Hilary answered for her, adding with irrefutable logic, 'You hadn't been away from people for *that* long.'

'Maybe Daddy found you a better job?' Steve offered, not nastily, but with a cynical emphasis.

'My leaving the research team had nothing to do with my father, and nor does he find me jobs!' she told him, furious that he seemed to have asked her here just to bait her.

'Not even this one?'

'This was different. It's a temporary posting, nothing more!'

'Stop teasing the girl, Steve!'

Hilary came to her rescue, but only, it seemed, to pursue her own line of questioning.

'Were you concerned about the work Martin was doing?' she asked bluntly.

Jo felt a panicky desperation building up. Again she took in the bleak practicality of the room, but it offered little in the way of diversions. Hilary's opening conversation and subsequent persistence had robbed her of any thoughts about interior decorating!

'I have a feeling Jo would rather not continue this conversation,' Steve observed, his eyes fixed on her face as if he could read her inner turmoil in her features. She threw him a grateful smile, although his own contribution had been equally unsettling.

'Oh, does it bother you?' Hilary asked, obviously startled by the idea that someone might find her probing too personal or offensive.

'I think so,' Jo told her honestly. 'I've never discussed it with anyone before——'

'And now this comparative stranger is bombarding you with questions,' Steve put in.

Both women smiled at him, Hilary with a slightly shamefaced grimace, and Jo with heartfelt gratitude.

'He's always telling me I have absolutely no tact,' Hilary confessed, and Jo found herself warming to the forthright woman in spite of her intrusive questions and irritating persistence.

'Well, it was coming from one who knows,' Jo told her with a touch of acid in her voice as she remembered things Steve had said to her.

Hilary chuckled delightedly.

'You're right,' she said, adding in an authoritative way, 'Go and get on with the dinner, Steve. You don't have to stand guard over Jo. I won't push her into talking about it if it upsets her!'

'I doubt he's standing guard over me,' Jo told her, as she watched the broad back disappear out of the room. 'He has all the subtlety of a sledgehammer in most of our dealings.'

'Oh, is that so?' said Hilary, the phrase carrying strange inflexions that Jo could not interpret.

'Was this a house before Steve converted it into his surgery?' Jo asked, relieved to be able, at last, to get the attention away from Martin.

'Yes, a little three-bedroom place. All he had to do was alter the front entrance and two of the bedrooms and he had a waiting-room, surgery, little office and flat.'

And two from three leaves one, Jo thought bleakly. This conversation was proving worse than the previous one. The last thing she wanted to think about was Steve and Hilary's sleeping arrangements.

'This is a dreadful room.' She changed the subject again, looking round at the plain bare walls and functional furniture. 'When you think of the beautiful things rotting away out there at Cooraminya, it's a crime that their owner should have actually bought this stuff.'

'I suppose you're right,' Hilary agreed slowly, her eyes taking in the room as if seeing it for the first time. 'The extent of my home decorating ability is to buy a huge number of pot-plants and plonk them down in all the empty spots. Steve tells me you're interested in furniture.'

Jo felt a surge of relief as she realised she had successfully diverted the other woman. With great enthusiasm, she rushed into a description of her activities that afternoon, cleaning and polishing the carved dining-chairs out at the old homestead.

'Dinner is served, ladies,' their host said, appearing like a genie in the doorway some time later. 'Come along and help yourselves.' The tantalising smell of curry had been fuelling Jo's hunger for some time. She followed Hilary into the kitchen where an array of plates and bowls were spread out on the table. They held a sumptuous variety of hot dishes and cold sambals.

'You're a genius,' Hilary said, giving Steve a quick kiss on the cheek. Jo's hunger turned to a faint nausea. It was one thing to decide with cool logic that she wasn't interested in Steve Hemming—any more than he was interested in her!—but it was quite another thing to convince her body.

'I really should have married you for your cooking ability alone!' Hilary was saying, while Jo examined the assorted dishes, choosing a little of each to test the tastes. As she arranged the food on her plate, she tried to block out the by-play between the others, feeling like an intruder in a scene that was meant for two. They carried their meals into the bare living-room, sinking back into the mass-produced armchairs that Jo had criticised earlier.

The food was delicious, and conversation waned as

they all enjoyed it, limiting their words to occasional questions directed to the chef, and comments about the flavours he had combined to such good effect. Replete at last, Jo relaxed back in the chair, silently savouring the pleasure that an excellent meal provided.

'Martin's research results have been questioned, you know!' Hilary said suddenly.

The flat statement brought her back to earth with a thud. She looked up to see Steve's eyes fixed on her face, their heavy lids masking his thoughts.

'She never gives up,' he said quietly, nodding his head towards his house-guest.

'So I noticed,' Jo responded with a twist of her lips that was part smile, part grimace. With polite determination, she rose to her feet. 'That was a great meal, Steve, and it's been a most pleasant evening, but I'm a working girl and I must be off.' She smiled properly at him now. 'Thank you for inviting me,' she added politely and received a nod in acknowledgement.

'It was great to meet you, Hilary, and I hope to see more of you while you're here.' She put out her hand, and, as Hilary took it she added bitterly, 'Questioning's one thing, proving them wrong might be harder!'

She was almost out at her car when Steve caught up with her, halting her with a heavy hand on her shoulder. Startled, she swung around, tilting her head to look up into his face. The moonlight threw it into shadow, but she could see his lips were compressed into a thin straight line, and his brows were drawn together in a frown. She was unaware that the same moonlight was shining directly down on to her clear skin, giving it a creamy opalescence, and highlighting the good bones in her face. It lit her hair to glossy darkness and cast shadows from her long lashes across the faint flush that was mounting to her cheeks.

She heard him sucking in his breath, like a drowning man gasping for air, and felt a tension building between them that almost crackled in the night air.

'Did you —— ?'

'Don't —— '

They both spoke at once, breaking the spell that had held them in thrall as they stopped, then laughed, then both started again.

'You go first,' Jo told him. 'I was only going to ask if you wanted something.'

Steve continued to stare down at her, studying her so intently that a feeling of unease began to creep into her bones. The hand that had fallen on her shoulder was still there, but the grip had become a caress, as the fingers moved against her bare skin, sending tremors of anticipation tingling through her body.

Did she mean something to him? Had he come out to see her on her own, to kiss her goodnight?

'Don't let Hilary upset you,' he said finally, while she watched his lips form words she did not want to hear. 'Much as I love her, she can be quite devastatingly blunt at times, and incredibly persistent.'

'I've got to go,' Jo muttered as her ears selected one phrase and sent it drumming through her head.

She turned and walked away from him, concentrating on the little movements that were usually automatic, as if turning on her headlights and pulling out from the kerb were the most important tasks she would ever have to perform.

'You're an idiot,' she chided herself as she drove through the deserted streets. 'You've known about Hilary all along. Apart from one kiss, he's shown absolutely no interest in you, so why are you behaving in this way?'

CHAPTER SEVEN

JO BLAMED her sleepless night on the curry, but all thoughts of Steve and Hilary were swept aside when she saw her first outpatient next morning. The little aboriginal girl was limp in her mother's arms, and Jo could feel the heat emanating from her body before she touched the burning skin.

'I'm Jo Armitage,' she introduced herself.

'I'm Helen and this is Amy,' the woman responded shyly.

'Well, first we must get Amy's temperature down,' Jo said calmly, lifting the little one gently and taking her swiftly into a cubicle, while calling to a nurse to assist her.

'Wet that towel and sponge her all over,' she told the anxious mother, hoping that the task would help to allay her fears. As she was speaking, she spooned liquid Panadol into the unresisting mouth of the baby. 'How long has she been like this?'

She examined the tiny body while Helen described the restless crying of the day before and the sleepless night that had preceded the rapid rise in the baby's temperature.

'Is there anything going around among the kids at the station?' she asked. 'Measles, chickenpox?'

'Not at the moment,' Helen assured her. 'Most of the kids, they have measles vaccine at two or three, so it doesn't spread so badly any more.'

Jo nodded. It was the introduction of the 'white man's diseases' like measles that had decimated the

111

aboriginal population in the early days of white settlement, but a widespread vaccination programme had
virtually eliminated at least one of the potential killers.

'What injections has she had?' she asked

'Just the normal triple antigens.'

'Did she have any reaction? Run a temperature after
them?'

The other woman looked thoughtful, then shook her
head.

'No!' she said definitely. 'She was a bit grizzly and
might have been a bit hot, but nothing more.'

'We'll put her into the ward,' Jo explained. 'She's
dehydrated and needs fluids so I'll put in a drip. All we
can do is keep her temperature down, and wait and
see. If it is measles, the rash will come out soon,
otherwise. . .'

'Otherwise?' Helen prompted, and Jo looked into
her dark, intelligent eyes.

'It could be meningitis,' he said. 'Have you heard of
that?'

'It's killed more aboriginal kids than anything else
since the measles stopped,' Helen answered soberly.

'Only if they didn't get treatment!' Jo assured her.
'There's a relatively new antibiotic that we can use,
and we can ensure that her temperature stays down,
which will stave off convulsions.'

Together they settled the little one in the children's
ward. Jo was grateful that the other three beds were
empty at the moment—and prayed they would stay
that way.

'You can stay in here with her,' she assured Helen,
'but make sure you lie down on the next bed and have
a sleep when she's sleeping. You've had a long night
yourself.'

She left the room in search of Rosie and ran her to

earth in her office, immersed in the never-ending paperwork that swamped them both most of the time.

'Is meningitis common among the aboriginal babies out here?'

'Fairly common,' she acknowledged, pushing aside her work and giving Jo her full attention. 'Think you've got one?' she added sympathetically.

'Could be, or it could be some other virus that hasn't shown its spots as yet.'

Rosie propped her hands on her chin and looked up at her.

'Are you going to test for it?'

'I think so,' Jo replied, making up her mind as she talked the situation over with Rosie. 'A lumbar puncture will tell us for sure, and will also confirm the type of meningitis so we know where we are. The needle won't upset the poor little kid much more — she's very listless, but that's lack of liquid in this heat more than the temperature.'

'I hope you're wrong,' Rosie said bluntly. 'There are about seven kids under two out on that station at the moment, and, although they have modern housing and all the facilities of town, disease still seems to spread through them like wildfire.'

'They probably have a totally different genetic immune system,' Jo told her. 'Keep your fingers crossed!'

She went slowly back to the ward, collecting the needle and slides that she needed on the way, then explained to Helen what she was about to do. The baby raised enough energy for one cry as Jo carefully inserted the needle between vertebrae in her lower back, and drew off enough fluid for her test.

She had barely confirmed her diagnosis, when a second child arrived, obviously distressed and in severe pain. Don't let it spread further, she begged some unseen fate, as she proceeded to do what she could to ease the little body.

By the end of the day, she was exhausted. The third child she had admitted had already gone into convulsions, and Jo dreaded the possibility of permanent brain damage as a result of the febrile fits. The sequel to the disease was often far worse than the actual infection!

As well as starting treatment on the children and ensuring that all were kept under close observation, she had the problem of their families to deal with, and was forced to adjudicate between mothers, aunts and grandmothers, as they argued over who would remain in the ward with the sick babies.

An anger that she could no longer control had kept her going. Now, waving away offers of food from Melly, she stalked into her office and phoned Steve.

'Rosie tells me that there's none of the new HIb vaccine available to us out here,' she stormed at the first sound of his voice. 'Is that department policy or what?'

'Whoa,' he said. 'Start at the beginning.'

'The beginning is that I've got three infants from Araloonga Station in here with meningitis. Aboriginal kids are most at risk; they should have been the first to receive the vaccine! They——'

'A lot of them have, Jo,' he interrupted calmly, 'although it isn't always easy to convince their families that it's necessary.'

She fancied she heard a faint hint of patronage in his voice, and the anger she had felt as she battled to save the lives of the three babies erupted.

'Rosie says——' The words were barely out of her mouth when he broke in again.

'Are you at home or at the hospital?'

'I'm at the hospital,' she snapped, frustrated by his inability to listen while she got rid of her ire and demanded explanations. There was a faint knock on the door and Karen's head popped around it, her brows lifted enquiringly.

'Then go across to the house, have a shower, and I'll be there. You can yell at me more effectively in person and the whole town needn't know about it.'

She looked across at Karen and realised, with an embarrassed resignation, there was sense in what he was saying, but she was not going to let him off easily.

'I'll see you later, then,' she said, coldly formal. Carefully, she restrained herself from slamming the receiver back into its cradle, as anger again threatened to overcome her common sense.

'Those kids OK?' she asked quickly.

'Sleeping like babies,' Karen assured her with a grin. 'I was just checking on you. You've had a bad day!'

'You could say that,' Jo acknowledged with a grin, 'but it's over now and I'm heading off home for a cool shower. Call me if there's any problem,' she insisted. Dismissing the girl with a quick nod, she rose from her chair and moved slowly around the desk, fighting off the feeling of depression that had succeeded her hot anger. Maybe she wasn't cut out for rural medicine, she decided, if little things like this could upset her so much that she forgot her professional decorum!

It was only as she emerged from the bathroom, wearing a light cotton housecoat, that she remembered Hilary. Would he bring her with him? The thought dismayed her. The things she wanted to say to Steve were not exactly private, but she didn't want the other woman here while she said them. Didn't want her here at all, she confessed to herself, if the truth were known!

She was still standing in the hall analysing these emotions when she heard his footsteps on the back veranda.

'I'm coming in,' he warned, and she heard the screen door swing to behind him. Would she ever get used to this aspect of country life where people wandered in and out of each other's houses so casually? she wondered.

Then he was beside her, his hands reaching out for her shoulders, and his blue eyes, full of concern, looking down into her face.

'Oh, Jo!' he sighed, a hoarseness roughening his deep voice. Without another word he bent towards her, his lips meeting hers with an anguished hunger that drew her out of herself so that she felt she stood apart, watching her body respond to this man with a passionate fervour she had not known she possessed.

His tongue, hot and insistent, parted her lips, seeking the sweet moisture of her mouth as if to quench a raging thirst. His hands moved from her shoulders, fondling her back, his fingers tracing the line of her spine, cupping her buttocks as he pulled her body to him, moulding her against his hardness so that she felt their bodies were melding together to form one being.

Her breasts tautened and grew heavy and she moaned almost soundlessly as her puckered nipples rubbed against his chest, demanding a fulfilment that she could not express in words. Her arms stretched around his broad back, clinging to him for support as the sweeping desire he was arousing weakened her knees and melted her bones.

His mouth teased and tempted, demanding a response she gave freely, then gentling suddenly as if to still the raging emotions he had aroused, before fanning the embers of desire back to raging life once more. Jo felt powerless, feeling her body quicken, again and again, as he inflamed her senses with a subtle mastery that she was unable to resist.

As one questing hand moved inside the thin cotton of her gown and cupped her full, responsive breast, she gasped aloud. His thumb rubbed against her tortured nipple and a sharp ravaged sound tore from her throat as sensations she had never known swept through her body, releasing a sudden moisture at the deep heart of her femininity as it throbbed with an aching need. Her lips clung to his as if trying to express her feelings with words she could not say or did not know!

Lost in the uniqueness of her own experience, she was startled when he stiffened and drew back slightly, so that her body no longer drew its warmth from his. Long, strong arms wrapped around her as if enfolding her in a protective shield and she revelled in the assurance it gave her. He lifted his head and drew a deep, shuddering breath, while she felt the ground become firm beneath her feet and her weight settle back into her body.

'This is definitely not what I came for,' he said, his voice muffled against her hair as his head lay heavily on hers, and his arms maintained their imprisonment. 'And I'm reasonably certain that it's not what you wanted to see me about,' he added with an amused irony reflected in his voice.

The flippant words reminded her of her anger, but it was gone, swept aside in a wave of sensual longings that had rocked her to the very innermost core of her body.

'Why haven't those babies been vaccinated?' she murmured against his chest, not wanting to break the physical contact between them. The smell of his skin was in her nose, and she tried to hold it there. The taste of him was still on her lips, and she savoured it.

She knew his response to her question was a heavy sigh, as she felt the exhalation of breath ruffling her hair.

'It took me months to persuade most of the women out on the station to allow me to do the toddlers, when the first vaccine for eighteen-month-olds came in,' he told her quietly. 'It's hard for them to try new things, especially when there's a risk that at least one will have a bad reaction.'

He was rocking her quietly while he was speaking, so that they swayed together in the hallway, their bodies still locked in silent communion with each other.

'Having done the groundwork, we thought we had it made, and let them know about the new vaccine as soon as it came out,' he continued quietly.

'Surely they couldn't accept it for one group and not for the others — it's the babies who are most susceptible!'

'It wasn't the mothers — we had them primed and ready! It was some overworked clerk in the Government Health Department! Like the "Fluvax" each year, the immediate demand is invariably greater than the initial supply, so there's always a shortage at first. You've got to remember it was only released four months ago!'

Jo remained silent, her body revelling in the close physical contact, while her mind followed Steve's explanation.

'The fellow in Brisbane decided to solve his problem by sending the first batch of supplies of infant vaccine to the places that hadn't had the one for older children. Of course, the reason they hadn't had it was because it either wasn't needed or wasn't accepted by the local people as a necessity.'

'Oh!' Jo squirmed uncomfortably as his words sank in.

'Oh?' he echoed.

She shrugged, and pushed away from him as his arms dropped to his sides, and he stood looking down at her with a quizzical smile twisting his beautiful lips.

'I'm sorry I took my bad temper out on you earlier,' she muttered, embarrassed by what she had thought.

'You didn't really,' he told her seriously, cutting off her apology with a feather-light kiss. 'I stopped your little tirade before you got started. What puzzles me is that Rosie could have told you this.'

'She did tell me something, but I must have taken it the wrong way,' she admitted sheepishly, remembering her assumption that either he or the health department — or both — were to blame for the epidemic that looked likely to spread through the native children at Araloonga.

'You often take things the wrong way,' he whispered indistinctly, his lips moving against her temple. She snuggled closer and raised her head again, eager for his kisses. The strident ringing of the phone jangled in the air between them and they sprang apart like guilty children, caught in some illicit act. She moved towards it reluctantly.

'I must go!'

Steve mouthed the words from the doorway as she listened and nodded, the receiver pressed against her ear.

'Just a minute, Dad,' she said and, covering the mouthpiece with her hand, she looked across the room at the man who was disrupting her life. Don't go, she wanted to say, but her lips wouldn't form the words.

'It's my father,' she explained, embarrassment tinging her cheeks to a rosy pink as she added, 'I fired off a nasty fax to him earlier this afternoon.'

'To your father?'

'Not so much a "Dear Dad" as an angry complaint to the director! Actually, now that I know more, I'm glad he is my father! Another boss might be less forgiving.'

Steve smiled, but somehow there was little warmth in the expression. It seemed as if this reminder of who she was, added to his anger about her appointment, had caused the magic of their meeting to dissolve into nothingness.

'I won't see you tomorrow,' he said. 'Hilary and I are going down to Yaroona for the weekend.'

Jo felt her heart contract and all the air left her body in a swooping rush, but she kept a smile fixed on her lips as she nodded a cool goodbye and lifted the phone back to her ear.

'Sorry about the interruption, Dad,' she said huskily, her mind following Steve out of the door, and her heart wondering what this man wanted of her!

By Monday, when she could reasonably expect to catch a glimpse of her colleague, Jo's confusion had grown to mammoth proportions. That two kisses could have caused such disruption to her serene stability she found hard to believe, but it was a fact.

Waking hours were filled with conjecture, as she tried to fathom out what both her own and Steve's feelings might be, and the nights were worse. She dreamed ceaselessly. Uneasy, haunting nightmares where Martin changed to Steve then back to Martin — mocking her, taunting her, teasing her, until she woke, drained and tired, her body damp and uncomfortable as unfamiliar longings were heightened by the tense duality of the nightmares.

'Did you pull strings?' Rosie asked suspiciously when they met for a quick cup of coffee before Jo started in Outpatients.

'Strings?' She forced her jaded mind back to the job in hand.

'A supply of the new derivative of the HIb vaccine arrived on the paper plane this morning. Someone's taken smart action to organise that over the weekend!' Rosie held her coffee-cup cradled in both hands, but her eyes met Jo's steadily as she waited for an answer.

'I did speak to my father on Friday,' Jo admitted, 'but I'd faxed him earlier.'

'Someone with your connections could be very good for rural medicine,' Rosie told her, a wealth of meaning in her voice.

'Rosie, that's a terrible thing to say!' she objected. 'As if I'd ever use Dad in that way. This was an emergency that would warrant the same action, no matter who the director was!'

'Maybe!' said her friend in a voice heavy with doubt. 'But that's not what I meant. I was thinking more of having an inside line to the man in power so that in normal father-daughter conversation he would learn something of the specific problems that face us out here.'

'Nepotism in any form is unacceptable!'

Jo's heart flipped as she heard Steve's voice, then sank at the implication of his words. She battled to school her features into a polite mask. The hairs on the back of her neck prickled with awareness, so that she could actually feel his approach as well as hear his cat-like tread.

'The new vaccine's arrived,' Rosie explained. 'It's

Alison's day for Araloonga so it couldn't have been better timing.'

'Why don't you go out with the health sister, Jo?' he asked, pulling out a chair and sitting down between them. 'I'd cover for you, and you'd have the opportunity to see the station and settlement. It's a great place!'

His physical closeness sent light fingers of awareness feathering down Jo's spine.

'You do have the odd good idea,' Rosie told him kindly, nodding in agreement. 'I was going to ring Alison to let her know about the vaccine. I'll ask her if she'd mind a passenger.'

Jo looked from one to the other. So often, in this place, she felt herself being swept along paths that were not of her choosing. Out of control, she admitted ruefully, her mind returning automatically to the enigmatic man who sat beside her, seemingly unaware of the torment his physical proximity was causing her fluttering nerves.

'I'll see who's waiting for attention, then check the wards, and, if there are no major disasters, I'd love to go along.' She pushed out her chair and stood up, glad to escape from this man who had thrown her into such confusion.

'Take your bag,' he warned her. 'There are usually any number of untreated injuries and small problems out there. It's too far to come into town for what they consider little things.'

He showed no sign of moving and she hovered on the spot, hoping for some subtle acknowledgement that she meant something to him!

'If we ever get two doctors out here on a permanent basis,' he went on, the doubt he felt colouring his voice, 'we could do a regular visit out there, alternating with Alison.'

Jo heard the words, particularly the 'if', with a sinking heart. He didn't want her to stay! Didn't consider that she was suitable!

'I'll look in on Josh, then be off,' he continued, unaware of her despairing thoughts. 'Ring me if you need me, Rosie,' he added as he stood up and strode, on his long legs, towards the door.

Shrugging off the waves of disappointment that threatened to engulf her, Jo hurried in his wake. Concentrating on her work had been the answer to her problems once before; surely it would work again.

Driving back through the flat black plain country, Jo felt decidedly better. Helen had told her a little about the property purchased by the local aboriginal community some years before, but nothing had prepared her for the tiny, self-contained township that was Araloonga. She had been surprised by its beauty, with the freshly painted houses set in lush gardens, and shaded by rosewood or pepper trees.

'It's the artesian water,' one of the locals had explained, as she'd exclaimed at the flowers and vegetables that grew in such profusion. 'Water, and the women with time to tend the gardens while their men are at work. They feel pride in the place,' the old man had told her, a note of deep satisfaction in his voice.

The other surprise was the obvious prosperity of Araloonga. It was a co-operative venture that must be working exceedingly well!

As Steve had foretold, there had been enough work to keep her busy while Alison administered the vaccine to the babies. Removing a subtarsal foreign body from a stockman's eye had been her first task, and, after

applying antibiotic ointment to the ulcer that had
formed where the grit was seated, she'd fixed a pad in
position and moved on to cleaning up a badly infected
leg wound.

'It's only an hour's drive to town,' she said to Alison,
as her mind continued its review of the day, 'yet none
of those people I saw had even considered coming to
town for treatment. Do you think a woman doctor at
the hospital puts them off?'

'Never!' was the prompt response. 'Most of them
would probably prefer to see a woman—it's more in
keeping with their own traditions.'

'Then why do they put up with the pain, and
encourage infection by leaving things untreated?'

Alison, alert for stray sheep or kangaroos, kept her
eyes on the road, which ran straight and flat through
low scrub and gidgee trees, but her forehead was
furrowed in thought.

'It's to do with their work, I think,' she said at last,
trying to explain these complex people. 'For so long
they've worked for others, but now whatever they do
is for themselves, for their own family and tribe. They
hate being away from the place; hate taking a few
hours off!'

'Steve suggested alternating with your visits, but that
really wouldn't solve the problem of regular care.
Would an evening outpatients clinic be the answer?
That way they could come to town after work,' Jo
suggested.

'You'd have to ask Steve about it,' Alison told her,
shaking her head doubtfully.

Dissatisfaction prickled at Jo's nerves and she wrig-
gled uncomfortably. It had been an enjoyable day, and
Alison was pleasant company, but she knew she
couldn't let her remark go unchallenged.

'Why?' she asked brusquely.

'Why ask Steve?' Alison looked at her in amazement, her eyes diverted from the road as she queried Jo's single word. 'Because he's the one that would have to keep it up,' Alison continued bluntly in reply to Jo's nod. 'It's OK for people like yourself who come in here for a few months and set up all these great schemes, but, eventually, it falls to Steve to maintain them, or stop them. One way he ends up exhausted, and the other he ends up furious with himself because he has to admit that he's only human and can't do everything.'

'What makes you think he'll be on his own after I leave? The department has already approved the appointment of a permanent superintendent at Warilla.'

'It's one thing approving the appointment, and quite another finding someone willing to stay,' Alison said sharply. 'We've had years of hassle over this, remember.'

'You sound as if you believe that anyone would be better than no one,' Jo said, a tiny ray of hope blossoming inside her.

'How bad could a fully qualified doctor be?'

Jo sighed.

'How much longer have you got out here?' Alison asked, breaking into her thoughts as she watched the green-grey landscape flashing by.

'Six weeks,' she responded and sighed again.

'Well, take my advice and don't get too carried away with new ideas. Unless Steve persuades Hilary to marry him this time, there's not much chance of getting someone out here when you leave, although. . .' Alison paused as she negotiated a particularly rough cattle grid '. . .they could send out another locum, I suppose. If we get enough people filling the post on a temporary basis, we might eventually end up with someone who actually likes the bush enough to stay.'

'I like the bush,' Jo said quickly, so annoyed by the cynicism in Alison's voice that she could ignore the jolting shock the other girl's first words had caused.

'That's not what I heard,' was the laconic reply.

'And just what did you hear?' Jo's voice was cold enough to startle Alison, and the latter turned her head to study her passenger again, as if seeing her for the first time.

'I heard you found Warilla boring,' she said defensively. 'Hilary told me! We weren't gossiping, just talking about how much easier it was for Steve with another doctor in town.'

'It's no wonder you can't get people to stay here,' Jo told her bitterly. 'Every word they utter gets broadcast round the town within five minutes of leaving their lips,' she continued, warming to the subject as she gave full rein to her anger. 'I thought hospitals were bad when it came to news spreading like wildfire, but this town beats their grapevines hands down.'

She lapsed into a bleak silence, her thoughts too confused to untangle. She loved the work she was doing, and knew, without a doubt, that she wanted to practise in a rural community. She liked Warilla, and the people she had met here. She would like nothing better than to stay on, but. . .

The 'but' was not going anywhere, and, while he remained here. . . Her thoughts stopped right there every time. The attraction she felt towards Steve was undeniable. Was it simply a physical attraction? After all, she barely knew the man! Did he feel something for her? Where did Hilary fit into the picture? Could she stay on here if he married Hilary?

She shook her head and sighed again. Of all the questions that chased through her mind, the last was the only one she could answer with any confidence — and the answer to it was an unequivocal no!

CHAPTER EIGHT

'HAVE you seen Josh?'

I should be used to the way this man treats me, Jo thought, as she looked up from the indecipherable scrawl on the letter she held in her hand. One glance at his thunderous face told her all was not well, and, what was worse, his tone intimated that whatever was wrong must be her fault.

'No,' she responded shortly, dropping her eyes back to the letter as the rapid beating of her heart threatened to overcome all other thoughts. How can his presence affect me so deeply? she asked herself piteously, while her mind tried to grapple with what he was telling her.

'The chemo drugs have reacted badly. He's been violently ill all afternoon!'

The angry condemnation still rang in his voice, as if she were to blame for the old man's discomfort.

'I've been back from Araloonga for exactly five minutes,' she told him defensively. 'I wasn't aware the drugs had arrived, nor that you were going to start on the chemo today.'

She felt her anger burning in her cheeks and snapping in her eyes. It wasn't only his attitude about Josh but this crazy swinging between friend and foe that threw her mind and body into a confusion she could not control.

'Perhaps, if you could possibly spare the time to fill me in on what's happened from the beginning, I might be able to help.' She glared at him, hoping he could hear the angry sarcasm that edged her words.

'Although I doubt it,' she added, as he edged through her door into the room, and slumped down into the chair. 'If the great Dr Know-It-All Hemming is confused, I'm sure an inexperienced, insignificant, *city* novice like myself will be no help at all.'

He raised his head and looked at her with puzzled eyes, as if seeking to remember who she was.

'I understood you'd worked in chemotherapy research with Martin,' he retorted, his voice as crisp and cold as frosty grass. 'Or was that just an excuse to be close to your lover?' he muttered bitterly.

She stifled the words of denial that sprang to her lips and swallowed the hurt anger that followed.

'Perhaps if you'd be good enough to tell me what's been administered, we might be able to discuss this scientifically.'

'It's all here.' He shifted in the chair so that he could reach into his pocket, and her eyes followed the movement of his long body, and her own body, unbidden, remembered its warmth! He found the paper and thrust it across the desk towards her, drawing back his fingers as she reached out, as if her touch might contaminate him.

She looked at the chemicals, summing up the dosages and the strength of the cytotoxic drugs and the corresponding dosage of the antiemetics he had dripped into the patient's body.

'If the oncologist prescribed this, it should be right,' she told him, shaking her head as she went over and over the list.

'Then why are you frowning?' he demanded.

Because you're driving me insane, she wanted to yell, but something in the combination of drugs was bothering her, and she could only shake her head again.

'I've got some notes over at the house, I think,' she said at last. 'I'll see if I can find them.'

'You'd better eat first,' he said gruffly, and she looked up from the sheet of paper to see him watching her with an indefinable look on his face. Was it hope, or longing? She turned away, unable to meet his eyes.

'There may not be anything there that will help,' she warned, 'but I'll ring you either way.'

'I'm not going anywhere. I've told Melly I'll be here for dinner.'

He must be very worried about Josh, to have left Hilary alone on what must be her last night in town, Jo thought.

'I'll look for the notes first,' she said, her mind on the file of information that she was certain she had brought with her, 'then I can read through them while I eat.'

She stood up and slipped past him, walking quickly out of the door, fleeing his disturbing presence with hurrying feet but an aching, heavy heart.

Jo pushed aside her dirty plate and reached for her cup of coffee, without being aware of either movement. Steve sat across the table, his hooded eyes fixed on her face, all expression hidden behind their blank blueness.

'Who did you use for this?' she asked, as she finished reading the last page of her notes and turned back to the script. The letterhead showed the names of four doctors, but the signature was an illegible scrawl.

'Peter Anderson,' was the prompt reply. 'He was in my year!'

He would have been, Jo thought despairingly, gulping at her lukewarm coffee. He and Martin, and he's using this combination as a result of Martin's research, despite the fact that the findings have been questioned.

It's another example of how small this world of medicine is!

As she acknowledged what had happened, her heart sank like a stone. How could she explain her thoughts to Steve, who had already prejudged her, and was so prepared to distrust her anyway?

'Well?' he demanded.

'I don't like the idea of these two here, when Josh is already on low-dosage beta-blockers.'

With her free hand, she pushed the paper across to him, and pointed to the chemicals she had highlighted in lurid pink.

'Peter was aware of his medication before he prescribed,' he told her angrily. 'He wouldn't have suggested anything as fundamentally wrong as that.'

His scorn tore through her but she fended it off, knowing she must try to convince him for Josh's sake.

'It isn't the combination of anti-cancer drugs that are the problem. I'm quite certain all of these, alone or in combination, have no adverse reaction with hypertension drugs.' She spoke quietly, her head bowed over her notebook, and her restless fingers drawing tiny triangles round the edges of the page. She sensed him leaning closer, as if invisible threads held them together — and drew them apart! 'It's only since the specific antagonists have been added to the chemical cocktail that these adverse reactions have occurred. They've been trialling it on lymphoma patients because their reactions are usually less severe and had been controlled with Stemetil or Maxolon after treatment up until now.'

'You're saying he's wrong?'

'I'm saying try leaving these out,' she responded tetchily. 'You can give him one of the lorazepam derivatives by injection or drip if he is nauseated after the next dose. It's worth a try!'

As always, his attitude was provoking her anger, fanning it to a small flame of fury that burned inside her, seeking release.

'Is this what Hilary meant about the findings being questioned?' he demanded.

'I don't know,' she told him warily, hating the condemnation in his tone and the feeling of inadequacy it engendered. 'I suppose it could be.'

'And you've got information on this and haven't come forward?' He was yelling at her now, his deep voice beating about her ears like the persistent drumming of a diesel engine, shaking her as it echoed through her body. 'You knew that the findings were wrong and deliberately concealed it. What hold did he have on you? What sort of a person are you?'

'I didn't prescribe this,' she snapped. 'Your precious friend did! All the boys sticking together! Because you shared your wild student days, and hung on the coattails of the brilliant Martin, you all seem to believe that he could do no wrong.'

She banged her mug down on the table, slopping its murky contents on to the white cloth, then mopping ineffectually at the mess with her handkerchief. Her fingers trembled as the rage burnt within her, but the man across the table neither moved nor spoke. Somehow, his silence aggravated her even more.

'Your friend Peter would have heard more of what's happened about that research than I have, and what's he done about it?' she demanded. 'He's supposed to be a specialist! He would have to know about the questions being asked but oh, no! Martin was his mate and mateship goes beyond common sense or honesty or decency or any of the other things that are supposed to be important!'

'Mateship has nothing to do with it!' he protested austerely.

'Then why did you use him?' she demanded. 'Of course it's all to do with mateship! You condemn me for using my father's influence to get this job — which I didn't! — yet won't admit to your own networking systems that are far more powerful than any nepotism!'

Her voice rose emotionally so that the last words came out as a despairing wail, but there was more she had to say. So much of the hurt and anger that she had kept bottled up for too long was now ready to come flooding out. Glaring at his impassive face, she flung her words at him, hoping that they might hit some weak point in his unyielding façade.

'And, if you must know, I did speak up — first to Martin, who accused me of being jealous of his ability, and then to the manager of the research unit. And who was he? Another Martin fan, of course, who refused to believe what I had said. He'd rather believe that I was acting out of spite because Martin had broken our engagement — that's the way men's minds seem to work!'

'There were other authorities!' he said without a tremor of emotion in his voice, and she knew that he was right. Knew also that she should have spoken out in spite of the threats that Martin had held over her head! The knowledge of her own shortcomings only made her angrier and she frowned at her inquisitor. No flicker of emotion showed in his blank face, and his seeming passivity fanned her raging flames of fury.

'You can tell your precious Hilary that she was right — that the results were questionable — but no one will ever prove it, and do you know why?' she yelled, her voice trembling with frustration. 'Because he simply removed the two troublesome patients out of the control sample of over four hundred, and substituted two others from an earlier test, so none of his "guinea pigs" suffered in the least, and his results could look neat and tidy!'

'And it's only now, when the use of these specific antiemetics is becoming more widespread, that some people are finally wondering?' he asked quietly, but she was too upset to hear the sadness in his voice as he added, 'Why would he do it?'

'Because he was too vain to admit he might have made a mistake. He could have recommended the use of the drugs in specific cases, but Martin wanted more and he wanted it immediately! He thought he could play God and wave a magic wand and make chemotherapy a wonderful experience for the world!' she said with bitter cynicism.

Pushing back her chair, she clambered to her feet. 'So there!' she finished childishly, as her throat thickened with an almost uncontrollable mix of anger and self-pity. With a muttered oath, she flung the coffee-mug across the room, relieving some of her tension and finding a dubious pleasure in the harsh sound as the heavy white hospital china smashed against the wall and fell noisily to the floor.

Without a backward glance, she stormed out of the room, her projected ward round forgotten, as the memory of the treatment she had received when she'd mentioned her doubts about Martin's work flooded through her.

The house, which should have been a refuge, felt more like a punishment. Solitary confinement for the offender, she acknowledged to herself with a wry grimace as her breathing calmed down and her pulse-rate returned to somewhere near normal!

Knowing she would be gone for the day, she had turned off the air-conditioning and had not thought to turn it back on when she returned for the notes. Now the heat lay heavy in the rooms, tempting her to return to the hospital, but she could not face Steve Hemming, nor any of the staff members who might have over-heard her tirade.

She stood on the back veranda, listening to the hushed shuffling noises of the night, and feeling the bright starlight work its familiar magic, calming her spirit and easing her troubled mind.

I'll walk over to Rosie's, she decided, then do a ward round when I get back.

Showered and changed, she dialled through to the hospital, unwilling to call in while there was a possi-bility that Steve was still about. The sister on duty assured her that all was well, although old Josh was restless. Yes, Dr Hemming had left, and yes, she'd ring Jo at Rosie's if any emergency arose.

Rosie's house was in chaos, as fourteen Guides practised making bed-rolls!

'Don't you just take sleeping-bags these days?' she asked Elise, Rosie's eldest daughter and leader of one of the Guide patrols.

'Usually we do,' she explained, wrestling with a recalcitrant leather strap, 'but we've been studying the history of the area and found out that a lot of swaggies came out this way during the Depression. One thing led to another, and we decided to try a 'swaggie-style' camp this year.' She shrugged her shoulders and waved her arm around the excited group.

Jo grinned, remembering the excitement of similar adventures when she was younger.

'You know swaggies had to work for their meals,' she said warningly.

'Yes,' Elise replied, 'but who would want us to work for them? If we tried chopping wood there'd be blood everywhere, and who needs wood chopped these days anyway?'

'Where are you camping?'

'Out at the weir, most probably. That's where we usually go. The only problem is there's no wood for fires or making a humpy, so it won't be quite the same.' There was a wistful regret in the young voice, and it caught Jo's attention.

Cooraminya would be idea for the girls' camp. She was off duty this weekend and could show them over the house, which was a realistic exhibit of the history of the area. If they wanted to do some work, they could help her with the furniture!

'What bright idea have you just had?' Rosie asked, stepping through the folded blankets and giggling girls balancing a tray laden with glasses, juice and biscuits. 'Here, kids, refreshments that swaggies only dreamed about,' she said, putting her burden carefully down on a small table. 'Come into the kitchen, Jo,' she added. 'We can't hear ourselves think in here.'

'Why not ask Steve if they can camp at Cooraminya?' Jo said, as they settled at the kitchen table. 'There's plenty of wood out there for their humpies and fires. They'd have to be careful, of course, but I'm sure it would be better than the weir. I'm off duty, so I'd be happy to go out each day and check on things.'

'Why am I asking Steve?' Rosie asked, her eyes fixed on Jo's face.

'You're a Guide mother, and I've just thrown a coffee-cup at him,' Jo told her succinctly. 'Well, not quite at him, although I was tempted. I hurled it at the kitchen wall instead.'

'May one ask why?' Rosie was chuckling as she pictured the scene.

'He made me very angry,' replied Jo in a tight voice, but the tension eased as she remembered the irrational outburst and she smiled weakly. 'Very, very angry,' she repeated.

'I think Cooraminya would be a great place for the kids. I'll ask him tomorrow,' Rosie responded tactfully, reading in Jo's voice a reluctance to discuss her disagreement with Steve. 'If you're going out there yourself, why not stay? They'd love to have a special guest, and would feed you — or is that what you're worried about?'

'Guide food I can cope with,' Jo told her friend, 'but sleeping in a bed-roll on the ground is a thing of the past for this old Guide!'

'Stay at the house. There are more unused beds in that place than there are in our hospital.' Practical common sense was the backbone of Rosie's character, and Jo loved her for it, but it made explanations difficult!

'I'll come home to sleep,' she said firmly, hoping that the other woman wouldn't probe. The old furniture at the house drew her like a magnet, but the thought of spending the night in a bed that belonged to Steve — and might eventually belong to Hilary as well — made her feel extremely uneasy.

They chatted on, Jo relating the excitement of her trip to Araloonga, and Rosie touching on highlights of her day at the hospital.

'I'd better go,' Jo said, when they'd laughed together over the Guides' completed bed-rolls. 'Steve's worried

about Josh, so I'd like to spend some time with him
before I go to bed.'

She walked back through the deserted streets. The
warm night air wrapped around her like a shawl, and
the stars lit the night sky to a deep, velvety purple.
Lights showed behind curtains in many of the houses,
and the muted sounds of television gunfire reached her
ears. Was it because a woman could walk in safety here
that she felt so at home? she wondered, breathing
deeply, almost intoxicated by the fresh, clean air.
Surely the vastness of the bush should be more frightening than city streets!

By the time she slipped into the wards, it was ten
o'clock and most of her patients were sleeping,
although the old regimens that had them awake at five
in the morning no longer existed. She checked each
ward and spoke to the night sister, then went to sit
beside Josh, reading his chart slowly and carefully as
she watched his shallow breathing.

His pulse-rate had not altered much all evening, but
his blood-pressure had dropped suddenly when the last
observation had been written up. Twenty minutes ago,
she noted, and reached for the tourniquet. Alarm bells
were clanging in her head, and the din intensified as
she registered a further drop and felt the uneven
fluttering of his pulse. She pushed the button by his
bed.

'Get someone to help you take him back to Theatre,'
she told the nurse who appeared in response. 'I'll
phone Dr Hemming and Matron, and be right there to
do the pre-med.'

She whisked out of the ward and hurried to her
office, her heart beating a rapid tattoo against her chest
as she tried to deny what her training was telling her.

She rang Rosie first. It was an unwritten law that she

assisted at emergencies, and one that no one would dare to question. Assured that help was on the way, she dialled Steve's number, and, when Hilary answered, told her she was taking Josh back into Theatre, and needed Steve here urgently.

If Hilary heard the curtness in her voice, she could make what she liked of it, she decided defiantly, as she found Josh's file and checked what the anaesthetist had used in the first operation. Hypertensive patients were always at risk during surgery and she worked carefully through the notes and made a list of what she would need to help the old man through the ordeal in front of him.

'What's happened?'

Steve burst through the doors of the theatre, his eyes going immediately to the still figure of the man he loved so dearly and whose life was held in the balance by the tenuous threads of machinery that were connected to him.

'I think there must have been cancerous tissue in the bowel wall. The signs indicate that it's perforated.' Jo felt a surge of sympathy as the colour drained from his face, leaving it grey and drawn. 'Do you want an assistant?' Her eyes left the monitor for a moment, and registered Steve's nod as Hilary, scrubbed and gowned, came into the theatre. The jealous pangs she had felt seconds earlier at the sound of that cool voice were swept away as she realised how much a second pair of hands could help in a tricky situation like this. She nodded a greeting to Hilary, then focused all her attention on the anaesthetic machine and the monitor that told her exactly how the old man was reacting to the drugs.

She was aware of the two doctors taking their places by the table, and the almost balletic movements of their hands and arms as they moved with Rosie, in a kind of muted symmetry, performing their tasks with calm, remote efficiency although the patient meant so much to all of them.

'One miserable little bit of tissue and it's caused all this!' Steve said some two hours later, as he stitched up the resected section with infinite care, while Hilary irrigated the area with a sterile solution.

'He's holding up remarkably well,' Jo told him. 'Can you double check that there are no other lesions?'

Three pairs of eyes fixed on her face, silently demanding an explanation.

'In elderly patients the first dose of chemo is usually the weakest,' she said quickly, 'so it may not have affected a bigger mass. You don't want this happening again after the next treatment.'

'If there is a next treatment,' Steve responded bitterly, the anguish in his voice twisting Jo's heart.

'There's no sign of any other trouble spot,' Hilary said finally. 'I'll close it up if you like, Steve.'

He nodded to her and stripped off his gloves, his hands shaking as the tension drained out of them. Moving round to the head of the trolley, he stood beside Jo, his eyes fixed on the monitor that showed the determined beat of his old friend's heart and the shallow rise and fall of each laboured breath.

'I'll stay with him tonight, Jo,' he said quietly. 'I want to watch his reaction to the antibiotics he'll need to stave off further spread of septicaemia. On top of the chemo. . .'

'He'll be sufficiently sedated not to know how bad he feels,' Jo assured him.

'But major surgery twice in a month. . .'

'You can only do your best for him,' she told him, her earlier fury forgotten as she pleaded with him to snap out of the mood of self-denigration that was colouring all his thoughts. 'Go and make yourself and Hilary some coffee. Rosie and I will tidy up here and see that a bed is set up for you in Post-op. He's best left there on the monitor for as long as possible.'

Rosie nodded in agreement, adding in a firm voice, 'Just make sure you get some sleep. Bells will ring if anything goes wrong, and there's nothing to be gained from brooding.'

It was two o'clock before she got to bed, but some instinct brought her instantly awake at five. Butcher birds were carolling in the gums at the back of the house, but the beauty of their song went unnoticed as she splashed water on her face, pulled a coat over her knee-length cotton nightdress and slipped her feet into her casual shoes, before making her way across to the hospital.

Steve was on his feet by the bed, staring down at the still form with a curious intensity. As she walked quietly into the room, he reached out one long brown arm and drew her close, holding her tightly by his side as he continued his silent scrutiny of their troublesome patient.

'He's going to make it, Jo,' he said, exultation bubbling in his voice. 'I was thinking we shouldn't have tried to do it out here! That I should have forgotten about everything else and sent him to Rocky where he'd have been in expert hands. I was feeling so guilty, Jo!' Jubilation vied with anguish in his voice as he sought to explain his concern.

Jo looked across at the screen, where regular rhythmic lines confirmed that Josh was stable, and should have a good chance of pulling through. With a deep sigh of contentment, she rested her head against his shoulder, drawing strength and comfort from

Steve's nearness, although she knew this was revealing a weakness she should have kept hidden.

'He's a tough old bugger,' she whispered, her voice husky with unshed tears.

'You do care, don't you?' he murmured, his lips moving in her hair and his arm tightening around her.

'All doctors care!' she retorted briskly, fighting the urge to turn towards him and feel her body close against his just one more time. 'Now, leave him to me and get home. I'll call if there's any change.'

She felt his hand moving against her arm and shivered as her body reacted to the impersonal touch.

There were footsteps outside the door and Steve's arm dropped quickly.

'I'll call in later,' he said abruptly, and left her alone with their patient and her own depressing thoughts.

CHAPTER NINE

'I'm CAROL MCKINLEY, the Guide leader,' the voice on the other end of the phone told her.

It took a few seconds to register! The week had proved so hectic, her conversation with Rosie about the Guide camp had been completely forgotten.

'Actually,' the voice continued, 'I'm not a real Guide leader, just someone filling in until they get someone else. The leader left town about two years ago and the pack was on the point of being terminated—that's the girls' word—when I took it over.'

Jo rubbed a hand through her hair and made a non-committal noise into the phone as the explanations continued.

'We've got permission to camp at Cooraminya and will be leaving here at eight tomorrow morning. Rosie said you might come out.' The voice sounded hopeful.

'Of course I will,' Jo told her, remembering her assurances to Rosie. She was drawn back to Cooraminya each Thursday afternoon, lured by the task she had set for herself and the tantalising beauty of the furniture. In moments of honesty she admitted another attraction—a need to feel close to Steve.

Alone out there, she imagined she could feel his presence. Cut off from him by the depths of the misunderstandings that seemed to flare continually between them, she tried to think her way into the mind of the boy who had grown to a man with a deep love of this little piece of the world moulding that growth. An uneasiness plagued her where Steve was concerned.

Could it be love? She thrust the thought aside. She'd been mistaken about love once before!

'Well, in that case,' Carol was saying, although there was obvious hesitation in the words, 'I wondered if you'd mind giving the girls a first-aid session. We learn it out of books, but I don't know enough to make it interesting. A real doctor would add spice to the lesson and I'm sure they'd remember whatever you taught them.'

'I'd be glad to,' Jo assured her. 'What do they need to know?'

'Just basics — bandaging, treatment for shock, snakebites, stopping bleeding, that sort of thing. Bandaging's the only thing we're all really good at, because they love tying each other up,' Carol added with a chuckle.

'That I can believe!' Jo said, smiling into the phone. 'I'll be out there by nine. It might be an idea to have your first-aid session soon after that, while they're all still fresh and alert. Later, if Dr Hemming is agreeable, the girls can have a look through the house.'

'Maybe there are odd jobs they could do to repay the doctor for his kindness,' Carol suggested, and Jo felt a quick flash of excitement shoot through her.

'Odd jobs?' she said quickly. 'You just tell them all to bring a polishing rag and we'll finish polishing the old furniture. I was just beginning to think I wouldn't get it done before I have to leave. With the girls' help, we'll have it all gleaming by Sunday.'

She was smiling as she put down the receiver, the depression she had felt all week lifted by the thought of seeing her self-appointed job completed.

At least I'll have achieved something during my stay out here, she thought, and smiled to herself. He'll have to think of me occasionally — if he ever walks through the house and sees his furniture in all its true beauty!

*　*　*

The day was clear and cooler than usual, as she drove out on the now familiar road next morning. Behind her, at the hospital, all was quiet, with no emergencies cropping up during the night to disturb her rest, and Josh, tough as an old boot, recovering at such a rate that Steve was talking about another dose of chemotherapy within a fortnight.

Jo sighed, then realised that it was becoming a habit — like muttering, 'Oh, for heaven's sake,' under her breath at inopportune moments!

He's affected more than my hormones, she admitted to herself wryly, nodding at an emu who seemed intent on racing her along the side of the road. She drove slowly, hoping that the silly bird would not suddenly change direction and fling itself in front of the car.

It veered away, its long legs flashing over the overgrown railway track, its filmy grey feathers bobbing lightly as it ran.

That's what I'll be doing when I leave here, Jo thought, dashing off at a tangent. Cravenly running from danger that I can't face because, like the emu against the car, it would be a confrontation I couldn't hope to win.

The cheerful greeting of the Guides banished all her sombre introspection, and she led them up on to the front veranda of the house, and quietened the excited dogs while the girls distributed themselves around on the timber deck.

Using them in turn as patients, she demonstrated the techniques they needed to know for their first-aid badge, then invented emergencies for them to act out and respond to, each one more hilarious than its predecessor.

'I do hope I never fall out of a tree on to a snake and need mouth to mouth, a splint, pressure bandages and a tourniquet to stop the bleeding, all at once,' Carol told her with a chuckle, as they rewound bandages while the girls made morning tea.

'They'll probably never need to put any of it into practice,' Jo assured her, packing the bandages away.

With morning tea over, Jo led them through the house, explaining how the kitchen had served as the family home until the 'real house' was built much later. Walking through the cool, shadowy rooms, the girls whispered and giggled as they took in the ornate furniture that told of a different lifestyle from the one they knew. Seeing the beauty of the pieces that Jo had already polished, they fell to their tasks with a willingness that surprised her, finishing all but the main bedroom by the time they stopped for lunch.

'We're going to follow the river course down towards the boundary fence, after lunch,' Carol explained, as they ate rough sandwiches and drank the billy tea the girls had prepared. 'It's an exercise to see how observant they are — different animal tracks leading down to the water, what variety of birds there are on the property, that type of thing!'

'I'm going to tackle the big bed-head this afternoon,' Jo told her, 'so I'll probably still be here when you get back.'

It was a fine intention, but the bed was soft, and its linen cover cool and inviting. Her next moment of awareness was when she woke from a deep refreshing sleep, hours later, the room gloomy in the gathering dusk, and the sound of the girls' voices echoing from their camp site on the high bank of the river.

Stretching and shaking herself to throw off the inertia of her slumbers, she walked across to the makeshift camp.

'We're collecting branches to make our humpies, Dr

Armitage,' Elise greeted her as she drew closer to the line of trees that marked the river's course. 'Want to help?'

She fell in behind the girl, following her under the low branches of a gum, and down on to a ledge on the dry bank. Knowing they would want supports for their shelters, she picked up a long, leafless branch, and was hefting it in her hand to test its strength when a gasping cry from Elise made her spin around. The girl was bent over, frozen where she stood, her hand outstretched as if she had bent to pick up what she thought was a stick. A brown snake was rearing towards her, its tongue flashing like blue fire as it weaved in hypnotic rhythm in front of the paralysed girl.

Without thinking, Jo raised her branch and struck, bringing it down on the sinuous body with all the strength she possessed. Again and again she hit out, beating the writhing creature until it lay still on the ground and others had gathered, drawn by cries that she did not know she had uttered.

'It's dead, Jo,' Carol said quietly, moving towards Elise who was whimpering, a raw note of hysteria in the sounds that she made.

Immediately, Jo dropped her branch, shrinking back from the instrument of death as if it might contaminate her. The tableau in front of her wavered as a faintness threatened, but the white face of the sobbing girl and her ingrained training brought the present back into vivid focus.

'Were you bitten?' she asked sharply.

'I think so,' was the tense reply, and Jo moved swiftly to her side, examining the arm that she held out.

'Do any of you know what snake it is?' she asked, her eyes avoiding the loathsome heap on the ground.

Indefinite mutters of 'brown' and 'tiger' reached her ears, and Carol shook her head helplessly.

'I'm a city girl sent out here to teach,' she explained briefly.

'Then we assume it's poisonous,' Jo explained very calmly, forcing herself to keep her voice as even as she could. 'Get those five crêpe bandages we were using this morning,' she told the girl nearest to her, easing Elise into a sitting position and holding the arm still. 'And you——' she patted another one on the arm '——get a blanket or cardigan to put around Elise. Carol, could you start my car and bring it over here? The keys are in it.'

She watched Carol jog away, glad that there were no signs of panic, although she was moving swiftly.

'You two girls——' she nodded to two silent observers who looked older and more sensible than the others '——find a plastic bag or something and pick up the snake with a stick, put it in the bag and put it in the boot of the car. The rest of you had better get on with your work, but make sure you look carefully at all the "sticks" before you pick them up.'

When the bandages arrived, she wrapped one carefully around the wound, tightly enough to compress the flesh, without cutting off circulation. Swiftly, she wound the bandages one by one, first down to the fingers then back up to the armpit, talking soothingly all the while.

'It is probably just an ordinary snake, but it's best to be sure.'

Elise nodded.

'I'll wrap it up just as we practised, then take you into the hospital.' Picking up a short stick from the ground, she put it along the bandaged arm and secured it with the last bandage to hold the limb straight and immobile on the drive to town. 'Do you have a special friend you'd like to have with you?'

'Can Amy come?' She pointed her uninjured hand towards the girl who was gingerly holding the main exhibit as Jo's little car drew closer.

'She certainly can,' Jo assured her, not telling her that she needed someone to watch for any adverse reaction while she concentrated on driving as quickly as she could back to the hospital.

She and Carol lifted Elise carefully into the car, then Jo took both Carol and Amy aside.

'Could you sit beside her and hold her arm as still as you can,' she asked the girl, 'and just keep an eye on her? If she shows any sign of having difficulty with her breathing, tell me to stop.'

The girl's wide blue eyes showed fear and confusion, and Jo hastened to reassure her.

'We must keep Elise as calm as we can, Amy, just in case, but we'll get her into town in time for antivenine to be administered if it is a poisonous snake. You can help by acting sensibly—just tell me to stop if you think there's a problem, OK?'

She watched the girl take in what she had said, and was pleased when she saw her straighten up and nod firmly, as she accepted the responsibility she had been given.

'Carol, could you ring the hospital immediately? Tell them to get Dr Hemming there as soon as possible— that way he can have the antidotes waiting, and, with any luck, he'll recognise the snake so we don't have to waste time testing the venom round the site. Ask them to ring Rosie as well, and let her know.'

She left Carol hurrying towards the house, and drove off, carefully over the rough dry ground, then as fast as she dared along the dusty road that led back to town. Intent on her own task, she was still aware of Amy's voice, chatting to Elise as if they were on their way to school, not on an emergency dash that could mean life or death.

There were tears of relief in her eyes as she drove up to the front of the hospital. Steve, Rosie, two wardsmen and most of the staff were gathered on the steps and the door was opened and the child carried inside before Jo could undo her seatbelt.

'We've got the snake here, Dr Hemming,' Amy was saying as she emerged from the car. The girl took the car keys from her unresisting fingers and went around to open the boot. 'Dr Armitage killed it,' she called after him as he followed the little procession up the stairs.

'Oh, for heaven's sake,' he growled, glaring at her with an insane fury in his eyes. 'Bloody city people will never learn. You should never, never, never try to kill the snake. Don't you know that ninety per cent of snake bites occur because some stupid fool tries to kill the bloody snake?'

Amy stood between them, mouth agape and the heavy plastic bag dangling from her fingers.

'Seeing you've got it, bring it in,' he told her harshly as he turned away and disappeared through the swing doors.

As if rooted to the spot, Jo stood there, tears of reaction streaming down her face, while her body shuddered with delayed shock. Abandoning her car where it was, she walked slowly and carefully around the building, moving with an automation towards the only sanctuary she knew here in this alien part of her land.

She had done everything she possibly could, and Elise's fate was now in other hands. That she would recover she had no doubt, as the antivenines were so effective. Whether she herself would ever recover—from today's trauma or from her time in Warilla—she was not so certain!

Reaching the house, she did not bother with the air-conditioning, although the heat was now oppressive. She walked inside and splashed cold water on her face, then shut and locked both doors, disconnected her phone and lay down on the bed.

It was a mistake. As soon as she closed her eyes she saw the snake, its twisting body and bobbing, probing head imprinted like a film on the back of her eyelids. Nausea overcame her and she fled to the bathroom where she retched uncontrollably for what seemed like hours, then lay slumped on the floor, her body welcoming the cooling effect of the ceramic tiles against her sweating, feverish skin.

'Jo, are you there? Jo?'

The deep voice came ringing into her semi-conscious mind and she huddled into a smaller ball, hoping that he would give up and go away. Such hopes were shattered as she heard his footsteps reverberating through the house as he searched for her with an urgency that she could not understand.

'Go away,' she muttered angrily, as a half-swallowed expletive told her he was in the room. Then his hands were on her, feeling gently around her, then lifting her with an effortless ease, to rest her in his lap as he sat, his back propped against the open bathroom door, his long legs crossed awkwardly in front of him to form a comfortable resting place for her body.

'Are you OK?' he asked, in a voice so mild and caring that the stupid tears she could not control spurted again in her eyes.

'I'm fine,' she said, her voice hoarse from nausea, and blurred with the misery that engulfed her.

'Elise is fine, too,' he whispered against her hair. 'It was a brown snake, and you did everything you should have done, and probably saved her life by acting so calmly and promptly.'

'You yelled at me for killing it,' she sobbed, not distracted from her misery by his praise.

His arms tightened so that she could barely breathe.

'Elise explained what happened. I'm sorry I yelled,' he murmured humbly. 'It's so dangerous to try to kill them. You could have been bitten yourself and. . .' Again his arms tightened convulsively, and his voice choked on the words as if the possibility was too much for him to contemplate.

'But I hate killing things,' she moaned piteously, trying to explain the extremity of her present reaction, as tears flowed unchecked down her cheeks.

'Hush now,' he murmured, rocking her back and forth as if she were a baby. 'Hush now, my little love!'

The meaningless litany soothed her, and the words of affection warmed her heart, easing the tremors of revulsion that had been invading her body since she returned home. Then some shred of common sense returned and she realised just how easily he could manipulate her with his tender talk and potent embraces.

She felt his lips moving against her hair and the memory of his other kisses triggered her despair once more. Kisses meant nothing to this man!

'How did you get in?' she demanded, pushing herself as far away from his body as she could, and struggling to escape his enveloping arms.

'I've got a key,' he explained, rendering her struggles futile with his effortless strength.

The ease with which he could restrain her was frightening, as she became aware of how vulnerable women were when pitted against the strength of most men.

'Let me go,' she said, panic shrilling her voice, 'and get out of here. You can use your key to lock up again. Didn't it occur to you I might not want visitors?'

'You're suffering from shock, Jo,' he said calmly. 'It was my duty to see you and make sure that you were OK.'

Duty! She stiffened at the word!

His hands reacted. They eased their hold on her and she felt foolish as she stood up and saw the dirty, tousled mess that he had been holding in his arms.

'I need a shower,' she muttered as he rose to his feet and hovered beside her. 'Thank you for your concern, but I'm fine now,' she added politely, hoping that he would go away and leave her to her misery.

'I care about you, Jo,' he said, a curious hoarseness in his voice, then he turned immediately and left the room. His words echoed in her ears as she pushed the door shut behind him, wishing she could shut him out of her mind as easily.

Stripping off her damp, dirty clothes, she stepped gratefully under the warm water, feeling it sluicing away the grime and sweat, and with them the worst of her memories, leaving her feeling cleansed, both inside and out.

Surely he'll have gone by now, she thought as she dried herself sketchily, hot air absorbing the neglected droplets of moisture that filmed her body.

She pulled on the cotton housecoat that hung behind the door, draped a towel around her shoulders to catch the drips from her hair and came into the kitchen. Any hope that he might have taken notice of her plea and departed were immediately dashed. He had teacups on the table and was hovering by the kettle, obviously awaiting her reappearance.

His hands reached out and grasped her shoulders, pressing her down into a chair. Removing the towel from her unresisting fingers, he stood behind her and rubbed at her damp locks, his fingers massaging her scalp and kneading her temples through the thick material. The friction of his fingers was relaxing, and Jo felt the tension draining from her body and a warm, sensual response creeping in to replace it.

'Go away, Steve,' she muttered, fighting against her body's weakness.

'Do you really want me to?' he murmured, his hands sliding to her shoulders and then down across her skin towards breasts that were peaking with desire.

'Yes!' she said with a defiant desperation, the word quavering as he bent and rested his lips against the softness of her neck. 'Yes, I do,' she repeated, as she felt his tongue flicking along the sensitive hollow beneath her collarbone, and fought the surging response as the blood accelerated through her body, flushing it with a heat that she fought to deny. 'I've had enough of you coming in here and kissing me, then going off without another word! I'm not some plaything sent here for your amusement, some toy for you to practise your kissing on!'

The words were the ones she wanted to say, but she was aware that there was something lacking in the delivery. It was hard to achieve the right degree of contempt when her breath was coming in short gasps and her body trembling beneath his questing lips.

'Tell me again that you want me to go,' he taunted her, as his hands slid beneath the thin cotton gown and cupped her heavy aching breasts. 'Tell me again,' he whispered, his lips against her ear, and his sweet-scented breath curling into its delicate coiling centre.

'I don't want. . .'

The denial was left unfinished as his thumbs rubbed across her taut nipples and she gasped, then shut her lips to stifle the faint moan that had risen, unbidden, in her throat.

'Tell me you can't feel the magic between us, and I'll walk out of here right now,' he insisted huskily, lifting her out of the chair with effortless ease and setting her on her feet so that her back rested against his acommodating bulk, while his hands continued their erotic exploration, and her body trembled beneath his touch.

'It's because we're thrown together in our work, that's all!' she said feebly, as she battled against her own will as well as this tormenting man.

'No, Jo,' he said, with an earnestness that penetrated her confusion. 'It's not that easy to explain away! I don't feel like this about Karen, or Linda, or Anne, or any of the other nubile nurses, secretaries and therapists that I'm "thrown together" with.'

'You must feel it with Hilary,' she muttered, the words bursting out with a vehemence she could not contain.

His hands stopped moving, and she felt his body stiffen, then he turned her around, and, with firm but gentle fingers, tilted her chin so that she was forced to look up at him, to meet those darkly blue eyes.

'Is that what this is all about?' he demanded. 'You're jealous of Hilary?'

'Why should I be jealous?' she grumbled mutinously. 'Your love life is none of my business!'

'I have never felt like this about Hilary,' he told her, his eyes holding hers as if to emphasise his words.

She felt her eyelids dropping as if to shield her

thoughts from his penetrating gaze, which seemed to be asking questions to which she had no answers.

'Never, Jo,' he repeated quietly, then his head lowered and his lips met hers and she was swept back into the fiery tumult that his touch could evoke so easily.

Her last shreds of will-power were dashed away as a joyous warmth enveloped her body and sent the blood fizzing and dancing through her veins, sensitising all the tiny nerve-endings until she felt she could absorb the very essence of this man through the pores of her skin.

His mouth demanded response, as if claiming her, branding her lips with its searing heat. Strong, work-roughened hands slid over the silken softness of her skin—shoulders, back and buttocks—lingering, cupping, stroking—rasping its heightened sensitivity until it burnt with a tingling, fiery need of its own.

Then those hands lifted and she could have cried out in frustration, but they moved to the front of her gown, undoing the buttons with fingers that trembled slightly.

'Undo my shirt!' The words of command pressed themselves against her lips as if he would not be denied. Her fingers moved of their own accord, driven by a will within them, fumbling open the buttons and pushing the thick material aside, seeking for the softness of his skin, the coarse roughness of the scattering of wiry, curling hair!

He pushed back her gown, dragging it down her arms so that it imprisoned them, pulling her seeking hands down to her sides as she tried to shrug it off.

'Not yet, my sweet,' he murmured, and held her apart, raising his mouth from hers, and moving backwards, so that his roving eyes could encompass her nakedness. Jo felt her body cringe, as if it feared what his eyes might see, and shame swept through her with a ferocity that made her writhe in his grasp.

'Does it worry you, my looking at you?' he asked in a hushed whisper.

She dropped her head to hide the burning flags of shame that seared her cheeks.

'It shouldn't, Jo,' he muttered, releasing his hold and drawing her close to the concealing comfort of his warmth. 'Your body is so beautiful, it fills me with awe and wonder.' His hands kneaded her back, his touch as reassuring as the words he whispered in her ear. 'It frightens me, in fact,' he added with an edge of roughness in his deep voice. 'Petite, and fragile, like a creamy porcelain figurine, so delicate, the blue veins shine through its fineness. Will I break this precious thing with my roughness?' His hands dropped her gown and spanned her waist, resting lightly above the jutting bones of her hips.

The words seeped into her numb brain. He thinks my body's beautiful! she told herself. He's not put off by small breasts and untanned skin. She raised her head, the delighted gratitude she felt seeking an outlet as her lips sought his once more.

'Bedroom?' he queried softly, and she could only nod, her head moving against his body, her lips on his neck where a pulse leapt and throbbed beneath the heated satin of his skin.

The room was dark and cool. He'd turned on the air-conditioning! She registered the fact with one tiny part of her mind that was still functioning. Then she felt the bed yield to her weight, and the fluttering touch of her sheet settling over her body. There was a jingling of coins, the soft sigh of a zip, and a rustling of clothes, then she turned to welcome the ardent body that moved beneath the sheet to lie beside her.

One arm slid under her shoulders and pulled her close, so that they lay, flesh meeting flesh, giving and accepting the myriad messages that words could not convey.

'Tell me you want me. Tell me, Jo, tell me,' he said with great restraint as she felt his body hardening against her softness.

She could only nod and move to meet his lips, silently pledging herself to the act of love that would follow — as inevitable now as the sunrise — and as welcome!

'Say the words, Jo,' he insisted. 'I need to hear them.'

She shook her head. Words meant so little at times like this, but she could not bring herself to utter them, knowing that, once said, they could not be unsaid.

'OK!' There was a challenge implicit in the single word and he rolled her back against the pillow, and moved his body away so that cold air wafted across her feverish skin, and she shivered slightly. 'We'll have to see about that!'

He seized her arms and lifted them, pinioning them above her head with the strong fingers of one hand. His other hand traced an erotic path across her body, moving with a restless rhythm that electrified her nerve-endings and made her bite her tongue to keep from crying out. Teasing fingers trailed up her legs, moving lightly against the silken skin of her inner thighs, lingering momentarily, then switching their bewitchment to her breasts, feathering lightly round nipples that were tight with pain.

'Please, Steve,' she moaned, her breath coming in a shallow gasp.

'Say the words,' he demanded, his fingernails tracing a line from breast to hip, to the tangle of curly hair, where they teased and twisted, touching the pliant lips beneath with a fiery intensity that made her try to twist away, drawing up her knees, but unable to protect herself. 'Then tell me you don't want me,' he whispered, moving his lips to her mouth.

Again she shook her head, and the torture continued, as his lips slid away from hers and nibbled their way down her throat, catching the low crooning noises she could no longer control as they pressed against her skin. His fingers had moved back to her legs, advancing and retreating across her skin, feeling her moist softness then pulling back until the torment became nearly unbearable. His body moved closer as his lips continued their exploration of her skin, tasting and testing as they followed a determined path towards breasts that were tight with a yearning painful hunger. His lips closed over her nipple and she felt his tongue licking at one taut peak, then sucking insistently while his fingers found the tiny centre of her feeling. As his teeth nipped at the throbbing nub she felt the engulfing flood of sensation sweep through her body, sending tingling tremors to her toes, and sparks of excitement shooting through her shuddering body.

'Please, Steve, please?' she begged, then gasped as she felt his swollen hardness pressing against her moist clamouring flesh.

His head lifted from her breast and sought her lips, muffling her cries. 'Say you want me,' he insisted, the words sliding through tight lips as he exerted an iron control on his body.

'I want you,' she cried in angry submission. 'I want you, damn it!'

She cried out again as he slid inside her and her legs wrapped around him and held him tight while her body shuddered its ultimate surrender once more.

Now he released her hands and lifted his torso off

her, looking down into her face, as he moved rhythmically within her. Her body responded, fitting itself to his with an ease and delight that astonished her. She seemed to sense what would please him and moved accordingly, finding such exquisite pleasure in the unity of their possession that little cries bubbled in her throat.

As if excited by the sound, his tempo quickened and Jo caught her breath as he carried her body with his, faster and faster until she swirled again into a mindless vortex, spinning out of control into endless space, riding on wave after wave of poignant intensity.

Almost drowning in her own sensations, she felt his body shuddering its own release and she held him to her, hearing the groan that was wrenched from his lips and delighting in his weight as he sank down on top of her, his chest rising and falling as he fought to fill his oxygen-starved lungs. Her lips moved tenderly across his sweat-slicked skin, delighting in the salty wetness that was unique to this man. He murmured her name, a breath of sound, like the echo of a prayer. He moved slightly, so that his weight settled on to the bed, but her imprisoning legs still held them together, as she sought to maintain the fusion of their bodies.

'Your leg will go to sleep,' he whispered against her cheek, and drew her over on top of him, so that she lay over his broad body, and nestled her head in the angle of his jaw.

'Do I take it that you enjoyed this little interlude?' he asked, as her lips continued to explore the strong column of his throat.

She nodded again, unwilling to trust her voice in the quivering emotional state that their lovemaking had engendered.

'My silent little love!' He bent his head to kiss her

hair, her ear, to nibble and suck at the fleshy lobe. 'I must teach you to talk to me, to tell me what you like and don't like, to whisper that my kisses send the fire racing through your veins the way the touch of your lips is exciting me now.'

His voice was hypnotic, murmuring about their love-making, detailing the touch that would thrill, the teasing teeth that would inflame their senses. His words emboldened her, so that, as her desire renewed itself, her hands grew brave and played their own games with his body, arousing his spent manhood to stiff impatience once again, and they took each other once more in a frenzy of excited thrusting force that left them spent and exhausted, panting lightly as their sweat-filmed bodies slid apart at last.

A pleasant lethargy stole over Jo and her heavy eyelids drooped over eyes that glowed with a soft sheen of satisfaction as she slipped into a sound and dreamless sleep.

She woke with a feeling of well-being, far removed from the tired reslessness of her recent awakenings. Memories of the night flooded her mind, and sent a surging pleasure through her body. With her eyes still closed, she recalled the sensations that the man had aroused within her, then flushed as she remembered her own abandonment as she'd responded to him with a spontaneity that, even in retrospect, brought a fiery heat to her cheeks. As she lay still, lost in her most private thoughts, she realised that her traitorous body was quickening again, eager for his touch.

He was gone!

She knew that before she opened her eyes, knowing that her skin would have sensed his presence if he was still in her bed. A sense of loss and loneliness threatened to overwhelm her. She wanted him; needed his reassurance!

The thought frightened her.

'You're behaving like a newly awakened virgin,' she chided herself. 'Wanting him here to say he loves you! It's the old "will he still respect me in the morning?" syndrome!'

The words, spoken only to herself but dreadfully insidious, rang round the room and she realised that she couldn't laugh away the truth!

She did want reassurances!

Her mind retraced the path of their arousal, and her mind confirmed what her doubting heart already knew. Throughout the tender touching, the exchange of kisses that deepened as desire fired their blood, not one word of love had been spoken. It had been a coupling born out of need; out of the physical attraction their bodies felt towards each other. Did their bodies have a knowledge denied to their minds? Had their bodies known their coming together could be so uniquely cataclysmic?

Jo sighed. She knew she wanted more from Steve Hemming than a brief affair, no matter how satisfying that might be. She was afraid to use the word love, even in her mind. Once before she'd labelled her feelings with that small word and then been proved disastrously wrong! She had five weeks! Would that be time enough to get to know him? Long enough to learn the truth of her own strange turmoil? Would he use the time to get to know her? Did he want to?

Her thoughts stole the happiness her body had been feeling but she forced herself to follow them. She must use her head! Hearts were too easily led astray! Steve had shown no signs of interest in her apart from the purely physical; made no attempts to learn about the woman behind the doctor. Did he still see her as the girl who had wangled an appointment to Warilla to escape the scandal of Martin's death? Did he still hold her responsible for that death?

Bother the man! His absence was more confusing than his presence! Then the memory of his presence returned and she wrapped her arms around her shoulders and snuggled down in the bed. He was on duty after all and would be doing a ward round later this morning. Maybe he'd come back then, to wake her with a kiss. Warmth crept through her body and she slept again, a tender smile curving her full lips.

CHAPTER TEN

STEVE wasn't coming!

Waking again at ten o'clock, she knew that with a certainty her heart could not deny. A cold lump of despair settled in the pit of her stomach.

Put it down to experience, Jo, she told herself sharply as self-pity threatened to overwhelm her. He had made no false declarations of love, so why expect more?

Common sense chided her bruised heart, but her body remembered the exquisite pleasure he had engendered, and she knew that it would crave more pleasure as an addict craved his drugs.

So have an affair with the man then walk away, her brain said blithely, but her heart contracted painfully at the thought. Casual affairs had never played any part in her life, not because she had unrealistic illusions about true love and fidelity, but because she knew she was not emotionally tough enough to handle them. When Martin had entered her orbit, she had been swept along in his wake like the shower of sparks behind a flaming comet. His brilliance had lit up her world, dazzled her eyes, so that all she saw was gloss.

'Of course you love me,' he had assured her, firing her senses with his kisses. 'Everybody loves me!'

He was right there, she remembered, lying in her lonely bed in far-away Warilla—loved him to the extent that he could do no wrong!

She too had loved that Martin!

It was the other Martin who had frightened and

confused her. The Martin who had needed so badly to be perfect that any small flaw in their relationship must be her fault. The Martin who had denied falsifying his records and had been prepared to blame her if she persisted with her accusations; who had lied to so many people — including Steve — about his work, and their relationship, yet been believed!

'Enough!' she said firmly, as dark memories threatened to flood her mind. 'I am not going to lie around in bed all day waiting for a man who might never come!'

As she walked through to the shower she remembered the Guides, and the house she had left unlocked at Cooraminya. Half an hour later, she was on her way, driving towards the place that had come to mean so much to her, to finish a job she had started. Her spirits rose as the flat plains and endless curve of blue sky worked their special magic.

He'll come tonight, she decided, and smiled at the thought.

Turning in at the gate, she saw the camp site was deserted, although the evidence showed that the girls were still on the property. A loud hail from the house led her that way, and she walked up on to the cool veranda to greet Carol.

'Have you seen Elise?'

A wave of compunction swept over Jo as she shook her head. Her own concern about meeting Steve at the hospital, about having to face him in front of others and act as if nothing had happened between them, had kept her clear of the place. She wasn't on duty, she'd argued with herself. There was no reason why she should go over.

Except for Elise!

'I'm sorry, Carol,' she said quickly, seeing that the other woman was watching her closely as if she could read the thoughts that had erupted in her mind. 'I slept late and thought I'd better come straight out here. I knew I hadn't locked up and wasn't sure how long you'd be staying.'

'I'd have made sure it was all secure,' Carol assured her. 'In fact, we decided you'd done such good work with the furniture that we'd finish off what was started. Come in and have a look.'

Jo entered the house with a sense of wonder. The heavy curtains were all pulled back so that light flooded the rooms, and the wooden floors shone with a deep, rich glow!

'Oh, Carol, it's beautiful! I would never have tackled the floors without machinery.'

'We had the next best thing,' the laughing Guide leader told her. 'Look!'

She led Jo to the main bedroom where four laughing girls were skidding around the floor with old rags wrapped around their feet.

'It's how the house is meant to look,' Jo said in a whisper, as the glory of the place and its shining furniture filled her heart with a harsh longing. 'It's like a home!'

'Maybe when Steve and Hilary are married they'll live out here all the time,' Carol suggested, unknowingly slipping a tiny dagger of pain into Jo's heart. 'It's not far for them to commute to work.'

'Maybe!' Jo agreed, and turned away.

She left the laughing troop and walked down to the river, following its meandering path while her mind puzzled again over Steve's behaviour. Her own response might be questionable, but his actions—for a man the whole town expected to marry someone else—were incomprehensible! Unless he was just an incorrigible womaniser—a man who had to prove himself by sleeping with every new woman in town.

Somehow, that didn't fit with the man she knew at the hospital. He was a caring doctor, taking his work far beyond the practice of skills. Then why was he behaving this way?

Stopping beneath a shady river gum, she let her mind run back through their social encounters. There weren't so many that it was hard to remember, she acknowledged wryly. He had definitely not courted her! Had not asked her out, brought her flowers or gifts, nor showered her with compliments—worthless or otherwise. It seemed, in retrospect, that he was drawn to her despite his feelings. As if he felt a need to kiss and fondle her, but did not want to, and fought the urge until it overcame him and he lost control. The hint of an underlying savagery in all their meetings could be the result of his disgust at betraying Hilary, or anger with himself for being drawn to someone he disliked!

So where does that leave me? she wondered, and turned back towards the homestead and her car.

I'm making too much of this, she decided as she drove back to town in the late afternoon. The Guides had packed up and left, and she had checked that all was as it had been in the house and round the camp site. Her natural optimism slowly took control. He would come and they would talk and all her groundless fears would dissolve away in the warmth of the joy they could give each other. And if it's only to be a passing interlude, then so be it, she determined philosophically, quelling the clenching fear that gripped her stomach at the thought.

* * *

He did not come!

Lying alone in the big bed had become a torment she could no longer bear, so, when daylight began to lighten the room, she was pleased to get up and face another Monday. Part of her mind accepted that there could be a reasonable explanation for his behaviour, but the other part insisted that, for a man who was rarely separated from his mobile phone, there was no excuse! One quick call was all she had needed; the sound of his voice to assure her that she meant more than a casual coupling to ease his libido!

Josh would be awake at the hospital. She would go and sit a while with him.

'Rosie tried to get you yesterday,' Karen greeted her, when she wandered over to the hospital before the night shift had gone off duty.

'Elise?' she asked quickly, her heart thumping nervously at the thought of disaster.

'No, she's fine, but old Josh died.'

Jo felt the blood drain out of her cheeks and a coldness creep through her body.

'When?' she asked, forcing her dry lips to form the word.

'Early yesterday morning. One minute he was sleeping peacefully, and then, by the next round, he was gone. Steve was out but we got him on the mobile finally. There was nothing he could do, and no point in waking you as well!'

His mobile had been by the bed! Why hadn't she woken? Why hadn't he come back to her? she wondered. Come back and told her, and sought solace in her arms. Did she mean so little? Did her own feelings for Josh as a person and as a patient not count?

'Steve's shattered, of course,' Karen was saying, the words breaking into Jo's tangled thoughts. 'Hilary flew up late yesterday, so he'll have her to comfort him, but. . .' Karen's voice tailed away as if the thought of what the old man had meant to Steve was too much for her to contemplate.

'I was coming to sit with him for a while,' Jo told her. 'He was always awake so early!'

Your Guide is awake if you want someone to sit with!' Karen said quickly. 'She's recovering so fast she'll be driving us all nuts before long!'

'I'll go in and see her,' Jo said. She needed something to do — anything to stop herself thinking.

If Hilary weren't there, she would have gone over to Steve's, if only to offer her condolences, but the other woman's arrival told her just who he needed in this time of crisis and underlined the shallowness of his feelings towards her.

With only part of her mind functioning normally, she was pleased to let Elise chatter, telling her about the visit she had had from the other Guides last night and filling her in on the rest of their weekend.

It was a day when all her professionalism was called to the fore, as she set herself to perform her duties while her body ached with an emptiness that she had never experienced before.

'You're upset about Josh,' Rosie greeted her, coming quietly into her office and slipping an arm about her shoulders, as Jo stood staring out of her window over the circular flower bed some hours later.

Jo nodded. She *was* upset about Josh, although her training told her that such things happened, and that, even without the treatment and operations, the old man could have passed away at any time. There was a rhythm to such things, and an acceptance of them that came with experience.

Just at the moment she was pleased that Josh's death

provided an excuse for her abstraction, as she did not want Rosie's motherly concern prying into her depression.

'I want to thank you for your prompt action with Elise,' Rosie went on, squeezing Jo's shoulders tightly as her voice quavered with emotion. 'If you hadn't been there. . .'

'Carol would have managed just as well,' Jo told her.

'I'm thanking you for more than first aid,' Rosie said with a quiet emphasis. 'I know how you feel about snakes! When Elise told me what happened I couldn't believe it! She was paralysed by her own fear, and would have been bitten again and again if you hadn't acted so promptly. You saved her life, Jo!'

'I hope that doesn't mean I'm responsible for her from now on,' Jo said lightly, trying to shut away the memory of that dreadful moment. 'I don't think I could cope with a teenager!'

'You can joke, Jo, but we'll never forget it,' Rosie told her emphatically, before moving on to the business of the day.

'Josh's funeral is tomorrow,' she said, when all their ordinary concerns had been covered. 'I'd like to go, and so would a lot of the senior staff.'

'I'll stay here,' Jo assured her, correctly interpreting Rosie's unspoken words. She could do no more for Josh, she knew, and funerals were to comfort those left behind. The only person to whom she could offer comfort had sought it somewhere else, and she had to accept that.

It was Wednesday morning before she saw Steve. She'd heard he'd been away for a night — out at Cooraminya, she suspected. He'd called at the hospital once or twice, but in the early mornings or evenings. Was it because he knew she wouldn't be there at those times?

She was back at what was becoming her usual post, staring blankly out over the bright flowers, when his big station wagon drove up to the front door.

I must get this first meeting over and done with, she decided. I can't skulk away in here every time he walks into the place.

Squaring her shoulders, she walked out into the foyer, her breath catching in her throat when she saw the bronze skin tinged with grey, and the weary redness of his eyes. Her hands lifted automatically, wanting to reach out and enfold him, to hold him to her body and murmur soothing words to ease his pain. But with a fierce resolution she held them by her side, curling her fingers into her palms so tightly that the nails bit into her tender flesh.

'I was sorry to hear about Josh,' she said quietly, her eyes fixed on his face as she dared him to look at her, to acknowledge her presence. Sorry you didn't tell me yourself—sorry about so much, she added silently, as he looked through her as if she were not there.

'I should never have undertaken his treatment myself,' he said shortly, 'setting myself up as an expert in something I know nothing about!'

'You did all you could,' she responded, as anger at his attitude and her own helplessness stirred her fighting spirit once more. 'This could have happened any time, with or without treatment, and you know it!'

'But it didn't,' he said bitterly, using an irrefutable logic to turn aside her condolences. 'It happened here and I was treating him and his last few weeks of life were so painful, so miserable that death was probably a release.'

'He was sick and in pain before the treatment

started, and the tumour was so large, he would have suffered more each day. He came to you looking for a chance, and you gave it to him!' Jo was trembling with indignation as she threw the words at him, furious that he would deny a doctor's duty to do whatever could be done for a patient.

'Could you two please have your argument some-where private?'

Rosie's head appeared out of the women's ward, and Jo realised how loudly she had spoken. She turned and walked into her office, but he did not follow and she felt an overwhelming sadness fill her being, as she knew that whatever had been between them had died with old Josh.

The weather changed, and heavy clouds rolled across the sky, pressing the hot air down on to the earth with a heavy insistence, so that the humidity sapped the energy and frayed the most equable of tempers.

'Have you applied for the permanent position?' Rosie asked, late on Friday, as they finished up their review of the week's work.

'No!' Jo told her abruptly.

'I wish you would,' the matron said appealingly. 'It's not too late. Oh, I know the weather's trying at the moment,' she continued, waving aside Jo's muffled protest. 'But it never stays like this for long. We'll get some rain then it will all clear away. Stay and see our magical autumn with clear days and balmy breezes, and all the country lush and green again.'

'Rosie, the eternal optimist!' Jo teased with a dry edge to her voice.

'You were pretty optimistic yourself not so long ago,' the older woman responded, looking at her steadily. 'It was one of the things I really liked about you, but you've changed somehow.'

'It's the weather, Rosie.' The excuse sounded lame, even to her own ears.

'No, it isn't! It started when Josh died,' Rosie corrected her. 'It's bad enough Steve getting around like a man whose life is over, blaming himself for the old man's death and taking out his bad temper on all and sundry, but to have you go sad and silent on us as well—it's just too much!'

'Is that how I've been?' Jo was surprised, thinking she had hidden her own misery behind her brisk competence.

'Well, you certainly haven't been the bright and cheery soul that first arrived out here, willing to take on the bush and Steve Hemming as well.'

Jo looked up in surprise, and saw the woman's shrewd eyes fixed on her.

'Was it that obvious?' she asked quietly.

'Only to me!' Rosie told her. 'He's the reason you won't stay on, isn't he?'

Jo nodded, the lump in her throat too big to swallow, as Rosie's sympathy broke through the barriers she had erected around her aching heart.

'Bloody men!' Rosie muttered, thumping the desk so that their coffee-mugs jumped off its surface. They both relaxed, their tension dissipating as they laughed together with the sympathy that bound them easing Jo's troubled soul.

'Come to dinner,' Rosie ordered, as she left the office a little later, 'and next weekend go down to Yaroona. You might as well see a bit more of the place while you're here.'

Jo nodded, then shuddered as a sheet of lightning lit up the room and an explosive bang shook their senses.

'Here come the rains,' Rosie warned.

'Do they always come so violently?' Jo asked.

'We often get storms. There's been rain further north and the heat plus the moisture in the air all helps to trigger these monsters.'

'I'll give dinner a miss,' Jo told her. 'There's only one place I like to be in a storm like this, and that's at home in my own bed.'

'In or under?' Rosie teased.

'In!' Jo answered with great dignity. 'I'll have you know that storms are one thing I am *not* afraid of!'

'Fair enough! Well, I hope you have a quiet weekend and I won't have to see you before Monday.'

Jo watched her leave then looked out at the green-black clouds that were rolling about in the sky, flicking the earth with their fire as they thundered overhead. The rain was still holding off, and the day had an eerie brightness, as if all the colours were accentuated by the unleashed power of the storm.

All through the night and into the day it rained. Not rain like she knew from the city, Jo decided as she sat on her veranda and watched it bucketing down from the heavens, drenching everything it touched and turning the ground into a slippery sea of mud. There was an untamed wildness about this rain, that brought life back to the bush with such a vengeful force. Dashing to the hospital and back became an adventure, and she felt a cleansing of her spirit as the clouds continued to tip their burden on Warilla.

'One of Steve's private patients has gone into labour,' the duty sister greeted her, as she shook the water off her umbrella in the kitchen at lunchtime. 'He said he was going out to his property, but I can't get him on the mobile.'

'It may be out of range with this weather. I'll see the

patient and you keep trying him. She'd rather have her own doctor with her, I'm sure.'

'I don't think she'll have a choice,' the sister replied. 'It's her third and I'd say it's due any minute!'

Jo followed her towards the theatre where all the babies were still delivered.

'If I were staying on here, I'd organise a proper birthing suite,' she told the labouring mother, as she glanced around the sterile blankness of the theatre.

'I've read about them in magazines,' the woman gasped, bearing down as she spoke and shaking off her husband's hand as she strove to bring this new child into the world. 'It won't do me any good; this is my last,' she muttered decisively, then cried out as the pains squeezed her body once again.

'It's a little girl,' Jo told her, only forty minutes later, then watched as the nurse placed the tiny, squalling infant in the woman's arms. Her eyes were misty as she turned away from the radiance on the woman's sweaty face, and the look of proud devotion in the husband's eyes as he curled a protective arm around his wife and child.

'I still can't raise Steve,' the sister told her when she emerged from the theatre, having seen her patient on her way to the private room that had been booked for her.

Jo looked out through the front doors. Although the clouds still hung low in the sky, the rain had eased.

'I'll do my rounds then drive out to Cooraminya,' she said, as anxiety began to gnaw at her stomach. 'I'll ring when I get there and tell you what's happening. If I haven't contacted you by three o'clock, you'd better send out a search party!'

'We could do that now,' the girl replied, but Jo shook her head.

'If it's something simple like he's out of earshot of the phone, he'd be annoyed by any fuss!'

She drove with a fierce concentration along the slippery road. One slight deviation and she would be on to the soft edges and hopelessly bogged within minutes. Two lost doctors would be too much!

His big four-wheel drive was parked at the side of the house, but there was no sign of Steve, or the dogs.

She rang through to the hospital and reported in. 'I'll have a quick look around and call you back,' she told them, her voice trembling as her concern rose.

The bike was gone from the shed! He could be anywhere, she thought, tears prickling at her eyelids as she sensed an urgency that would not be denied.

A sudden hysterical barking drew her outside, and there on the veranda a sodden dog yelped frantically, barking at her then running towards the river, then running back to bark again.

'Dogs only do this in movies,' she told the excited animal crossly, as she hurried after him, ignoring the rain that had drenched her clothes before she had gone two paces.

Approaching the steep crossing, she heard the other dogs, their voices joining in chorus with the one that led her on. The track down into the riverbed was a wet slide of mud, and water was flowing swiftly at the base of it, but her eyes were drawn to the huddled bundle of clothes that lay beside the heavy bike only inches above the rising waters.

The dogs watched her in silence as she slithered down to Steve, and felt frantically for a pulse. It was beating strongly, and she uttered a silent prayer of thanks, as she pulled off her shirt and mopped his mud-slicked face with it, examining the still white features for signs of injury.

She could find no mark — no swelling or depression around his head — but his eyes told her he was deeply unconscious. Leaving him on his side, she felt his limbs, her fingers shaking and tears mingling with the rain as she took stock.

His leg was broken, a compound fracture, the displaced end of bone sticking sickeningly through his ripped trousers and torn skin, but he'd been conscious at some time and bound his handkerchief around it to stop the bleeding, then passed out from the pain, most probably. Was that all? She could not tell.

'Stay here with him,' she told the dogs. 'I'll phone for help.'

They looked at her, their brown eyes full of trust, and whined when she moved away, making her way carefully up the slippery slope. The water in the riverbed was rising swiftly, and Steve's words about the floods sweeping down from the north drummed in her ears. It had been raining for weeks up towards the Gulf, and towns further up the river had already experienced heavy flooding. She could ring for help, but could she afford to wait until it got here?

Safe at the top of the bank, she ran to the house, where she called the hospital and let them know what she had found.

'Tell the ambulance to follow the track to the river crossing. Steve's wagon will be parked at the top so they can't miss the spot.'

Grabbing the sheet off the divan in the kitchen and an old walking stick that must have belonged to his grandfather, she went back outside, racing across the wet ground to her car, to pick up her bag. Steve's was probably in his car, but she knew for certain there was morphine in hers, and that was all she'd need.

Climbing up into his car, she took a deep breath,

and rehearsed what she had to do, then started it up, thankful that trusting country people invariably left their keys in the ignition. Carefully, she manoeuvred the big vehicle through the slippery mud to the top of the crossing, then hurried out, bag in one hand, and grabbed the winch cable, hauling it down the slope behind her until she was back beside his inert body.

Ignoring the water that had crept higher and now washed around her feet, she struggled with his clothes, seeking muscle she could inject the pain-killer into. Her fingers were no match for the wet material, and the rising water frightened her. Pushing aside his coat, she jabbed the needle through his trousers and hoped it had entered the strong muscles of his thigh. It would take a while to work, but should ease the pain he would feel as he was moved later. Right now, she'd prefer he stayed unconscious, she thought as she shoved the metal hook of the winch cable through the tag at the back of Steve's heavy oilskin coat, then knotted the rainhood around the cable to reinforce the join. Tearing the sheet into strips, she bound the broken leg to his good leg, padding the walking stick with her wet shirt and using it as a splint between them.

He groaned as she rolled him on to his back, and his legs splashed in the water that now reached up to his waist, but he did not regain consciousness. With fingers that shook, she did up all his coat buttons, and crossed her fingers for luck. The coat should pull away from him slightly when she pressed the switch, so the back of his head would be protected by the heavy flap that fell from the shoulder seams. Looking down at her handiwork, she took a moment to think through her next move.

'Just pray he has no spinal injuries, and that Drizabone coats are as tough as people say they are,' she told the dogs who had sat and watched her efforts with evident interest.

She clambered back up the slippery slope, following the cable and clearing its path of any sticks or rough stones as she went. At least the muddy surface should make it easier to drag him, she decided, as a thunderous roaring beat on her ears.

More thunder, so more rain, she thought fleetingly, then hurried to the switch that would activate the winch. Sick fear gripped her stomach as she realised the consequences her action could have, but the water was rising faster and the roaring noise she had heard was getting louder as if some raging beast were coming closer and closer.

She flicked the little metal knob and held her breath as the wire rope began to coil back around its drum. The dogs' noises grew closer and she saw the heavy body slide clumsily over the top of the bank. She threw the switch to 'off' and raced to his side, frightened by his white face which gleamed wetly as if pain had drained away his vibrant life.

'I hope you realise I've broken all my fingernails rescuing you,' she told him fiercely, as she tried to undo the knot that had tightened round the winch cable. Then she heard the wailing sirens of the ambulance above the thundering noise that grew more ominous every moment, and relief surged through her.

'Well, well, well!' Ned, the senior ambulance driver, stood looking down at her patient for a moment before tucking a silver space blanket around his wet form.

'I can't get the coat undone from the winch cable,' Jo said tightly, as if to explain the tears that still streaked down her face.

'We can pull him out of it or cut him free — either way he'll not be too pleased at what you've done to his good coat!' Ned told her with a warning shake of his head. 'Get a sharp blade, Tim; we'll cut it; that's the river coming down by sounds of things.'

He turned back to Jo. 'I'll tell him you cut the coat,' he said with a grin. 'Where was he?'

She pointed down the bank. 'The bike's still there and my bag; I'd better get them!' but as she turned away Ned's hand reached out and grabbed her shoulder.

'Let them go, lass,' he said. 'You can't go back down there, and the sooner we're all away from this place, the better pleased I'll be. Can't you hear the river?'

She looked at him in surprise. 'That's the river making that noise?'

'It is, and it's close! The road between here and town runs by it further down, so we'd best be going.'

Tim had brought the stretcher, and was cutting through the tough oilskin hood while they were speaking, and all the time the noise thundered in their ears.

'You run this car back to the house while we load him in and strap him down,' Ned told her. 'It doesn't flood there so it'll be safe. We'll pick you up and you can ride back with us.'

'I've got my car here, I'll drive that back,' she said quickly, confused by something in Ned's voice that was frightening her. He led her round to the door of the station wagon, and held it open while she climbed in.

'You'll come back with us,' he said, his eyes fixed on her face and a note of quiet authority in his voice. 'Get anything you need out of the cars then lock them and leave the keys in the house. See the dogs have got plenty of food, lock up the house and wait till we get there.' There was a pause for a second before he added, his eyes turning towards the back of the vehicle where Tim had signalled he'd freed their patient, 'And

I'd have a quick look around and see if Steve's got a shirt you could pull on. You're very wet!'

He slammed the door and walked away, giving the bonnet a thump to let her know she could back off. Her cheeks burned as the significance of his parting remark sank in and she looked down at the wet white bra which was all she had on above the waist.

She followed Ned's instructions to the letter, although she did not understand the reason for his concern. When the ambulance swung to a standstill beside her, they opened the front door but she shook her head.

'I'll ride in the back with Steve,' she said firmly, wanting to see for herself that he was still breathing.

He lay so still under the silver covering that she reached out for his hand, wanting its warmth to reassure her that there was still life in that strong body. The ambulance was moving swiftly, its cabin swaying as it slid in the winding ribbon of mud that had been the road. As they pulled on to a rise not far from the homestead, Ned called to her.

'Look back,' he said. 'You'll see what the river can look like when she's coming down! Tim, you get on to the hospital and tell them we're ahead of the water and will be there in twenty minutes.'

Jo peered out through the dark one-way glass and was stupefied as a sea of yellow-brown water raged towards then past them, sweeping tree-trunks as big as telegraph posts along in front of it, while debris of every description tumbled and roiled in its turbulent all-encompassing progress. The awe she felt at the sight of such destructive natural force was supplanted by a shudder of horror as she realised that this was what had been approaching them, warning them with its loud clamouring voice.

Her hand tightened convulsively on Steve's and she felt a slight answering pressure. The scene outside was forgotten as she spun back to look at him, to see the blue eyes, still darkened by the shadows of pain, staring at her with a kind of wonder.

'Oh, for heaven's sake,' he greeted her weakly. 'How did you do it?' he added as if he had no doubt that it was she who had rescued him.

'I winched you up,' she said with a grin. The happiness she felt, seeing him twist uncomfortably, and hearing him speak, brought a glow to her eyes and a shining pinkness to her cheeks.

'Some city slicker!' he said, squeezing her hand so tightly that she winced at the pressure. 'Jo?' His voice was deep and husky, edged with strain.

'You'll be fine,' she whispered, thinking he sought reassurance from her.

'I won't, you know,' he said quietly. 'Not until I've apologised to you.'

The stupid tears that her panic had started earlier prickled again behind her eyes and she looked down at her feet to hide her chagrin. Surely he wasn't going to hurt her more by apologising for his behaviour? How could he cheapen what had occurred between them by apologising?

'I've behaved so badly,' he murmured, 'and my only excuse was that I was more upset than I could believe by Josh's death. You tried to comfort me and I turned away from you, but I felt so guilty, Jo. Guilty because I was wrapped up in my own selfish pleasure while my old friend died.'

'Is that all it was to you?' she asked, her voice a silken whisper in the sterile air. 'A little bit of selfish pleasure?'

All the pain and bitterness of the past week came

flooding back, as turbulent and destructive as the waters she had watched rush past outside the window.

'Of course not,' he groaned. 'Do you think that a physical act could be as magical as that if real emotions aren't involved? Can you deny that our liking for each other, and other things, like respect and tenderness, were present in your bed that night?'

'And love?' she asked, aware that she was pushing him but unable to live with uncertainty any longer. 'Was love there?'

'My love was, Jo,' he said in a voice that broke and faded into a husky whisper.

Unable to believe what her ears had heard, she looked up and saw his eyes watching her intently, and a strange little smile twisting his lips.

'The last thing I intended to do was to fall in love with a pert little city doctor who'd been sent up here to get her away from a bit of scandal! But the woman I thought was coming and the one who came were two entirely different people!'

'A bad bit of prejudgement, Dr Hemming?' she teased as happiness began to stir within her, brushing aside all the pain, the loneliness and the despair.

'So bad I couldn't bring myself to admit it,' he replied, his fingers clinging tightly to hers as if they, too, sought her forgiveness. 'Then, just when I thought we might have found each other, when I began to hope that you might like the bush and be prepared to stay here, Josh died, and I felt so inadequate, Jo. . . I felt I couldn't offer you a failure. I thought you'd go away, forget about me! That it would be better that way!'

Those blue eyes, no longer hooded, but weary and full of doubt, clung to hers, seeking reassurances she was afraid to give — yet.

'You know I've pumped you full of morphine,' she

said lightly. 'It's probably the euphoria of that that's bringing all these true confessions to your lips.'

The heavy lids dropped to hide the sudden shock of what he took to be a rebuff, but they lifted again to say, 'It makes them no less true, Jo.'

What did it mean? she wondered as her mind swung wildly between its own euphoria and sickening doubt.

They pulled up smoothly at the hospital and the rear doors swung open. Rosie came running down the stairs and took one look at the dishevelled doctor who sprang quickly down.

'Slip home and have a shower and something hot to drink,' she ordered. 'We just happen to have Dave Purvis here. He was driving back from holidays and the floods stopped him, so he called at Steve's then here, looking for him, and was with me when Tim's call came through.'

'Oh, Rosie, that's wonderful,' Jo whispered huskily, her eyes awash again, although this time with tears of relief. 'His leg's a mess. I was dreading having to set it. I'll be right back.'

'Don't hurry; he'll be out to it before you get here. You're better resting for a while so you can be with him when he wakes up. Dave and I will manage.'

'He's had ten milligrams of morphine, tell Dave.'

'Will you stop worrying and go? With Steve out of action, you're going to be a very busy lady for the next few weeks, so you'll have to take good care of yourself!'

Rosie pushed her towards the path that led around the sprawling old building, and, suddenly aware of her sodden hair and skin, and the old blue shirt of Steve's that flapped about her thighs, Jo broke into a brisk trot, glad to escape before anyone else saw her.

The thick cloud cover had brought an early darkness to the late afternoon when she finally trekked back

across the wet grounds to the hospital. She had showered and eaten, but had not rested. The new mother
should be checked and she was due to do another
round. Rosie's words had reminded her of her
responsibilities.

'I guess you'll be staying on!' a laughing voice said
as she pushed through the door into the kitchen.

Dave and Rosie were sitting at the table, their hands
curled about their teacups, triumphant grins plastered
across their faces, and delighted chuckles bubbling on
their lips.

'What do you mean?' she demanded suspiciously,
wondering what had caused this sudden burst of good
spirits when they should be showing concern about
Steve and his leg.

'Well if you're going to marry old Steve, you'll be
staying on,' Dave repeated. 'He certainly won't be
moving anywhere else.'

She felt the blood rush to her face, and she stamped
her foot at them as she summoned up anger to cover
her embarrassment.

'What on earth are you talking about, Dave? Who
said anything about my marrying Steve? Is this the
latest piece of Warilla gossip? Has it just supplanted
the Steve and Hilary stories that have been going
around ever since I hit town?'

She moved across to the table and steadied herself
with her hands on the edge of it, while she glowered
down at the pair of them.

'You didn't fall for all those Steve and Hilary stories,
did you?' Rosie demanded to know. 'That was gossip
Steve encouraged so the town stopped trying to pair
him off with every single woman for a radius of three
hundred miles! I often think he asked Hilary up in the

first place to stop the matchmaking! They were friends at university but that's all.'

She smiled at Jo but must have realised her listener remained unconvinced. 'I should know, Jo,' she added forcefully. 'It was my fold-up bed he borrowed whenever Hilary came to town!'

'And I'm the new protection, the new "interest" to save him from matchmakers?' Jo asked quietly, her anger swept away by a strange relief that had flooded her body.

'It's not gossip, is it, Rosie?' Dave said plaintively. 'We got it from the horse's mouth!'

And once again they dissolved into gales of laughter.

'Oh, Jo! I'm sorry,' Rosie said at last, wiping tears of mirth from her eyes. 'We shouldn't be teasing you but it was so funny, and it's made me so happy. You will marry him, won't you?'

'He hasn't asked me, Rosie,' Jo told her bleakly, still totally confused by the behaviour of these two usually responsible friends.

'But he has, that's just the point!' Rosie tried to explain, although her chuckles were again impeding the words. 'He did it so beautifully — as if he'd been practising for weeks — but it was Dave whose hand he held, and Dave, not you, beside the bed.'

'"Tell me you'll marry me," he said,' Dave told her, '"Tell me, Jo, tell me!"'

The words rang in her ears and echoes of another demand authenticated them in her mind. 'Tell me you want me. Tell me, Jo, tell me,' he had said!

'And did you answer him?' she asked, her cool voice hiding the inner churning of her stomach and the fiery excitement that she could not control as it sang its way through her veins.

'I did,' Rosie said cheerfully. 'I said, "Yes, darling,

of course I will." I thought my voice was better than Dave's but Steve was so restless I was worried he wouldn't go under until he'd heard your reply.'

'But it wasn't my reply, ' she whispered.

'Maybe not! But don't bother telling me it's not what you would have said. Honestly, Blind Freddy would have seen what's been happening between you two! It's just that you've both been too stubborn to admit it! Someone had to do something about it, so go and do your ward round then sit with your fiancé. You never know what other sweet things he might say under the influence of drugs before he wakes up and reverts to his tight-lipped old self!'

Tight-lipped indeed, she thought to herself as she hurried away. Rosie didn't know him half as well as she thought she did. The memory of the words that had passed between them on that one ecstatic night of love came back to comfort her, as she accepted, with an understanding that was part of every cell in her body, that the uneasy, uncomfortable, ruffled sensation she felt when she was away from Steve, and the familiar, safe sureness she felt when he was near, were all part of this magical thing called love.

'Did I propose to you?'

The hushed words startled her out of her reverie.

'No,' she said with a tenderly teasing smile, 'you proposed to Dave!'

'Did he accept?' he asked, his eyes fixed on hers with love shining luminously in their blue depths.

'No, but Rosie did,' Jo told him. 'She felt you needed reassurance.'

'She wasn't wrong,' he said with a heartfelt groan, reaching out to clasp her hand in both of his. 'I know I've made a mess of this, right from the beginning, Jo, but you threw me into total confusion. You stood there in the doorway of the theatre with a huge gown bundled round your slim figure and your brown eyes looking up at me, so calm and wide and serious, like a little girl playing at grown-ups.'

His hands tightened convulsively but she remained silent, knowing that there was more he had to say.

'I knew what Martin had said about you, and I suspected your father had been responsible for getting you the job. But seeing you, watching you work, your care for everyone — things just didn't add up, which made my confusion worse. All I knew for sure was that it was as if I'd been struck by a physical force; the sensation was so strong that afterwards. . .well, I had to fight it, didn't I?'

His eyes held a gleam of self-mockery, as they met then held hers.

'Because you didn't like me?'

'I said that, didn't I? Oh, Jo, I am sorry. I was afraid of frightening you as badly as my reaction had frightened me. I thought I might scare you away if I rushed into anything. And then, of course, with Josh's chemo, you put me straight about Martin, and I saw for myself how you handled your father, so I knew then that my doubts had no foundation; that you were a good doctor.'

'And you needed a second doctor in Warilla?'

'Not as much as I needed you,' he confessed. 'It ate away at me, until I could barely think for images of you dancing across my mind! I asked you out and you refused me, then went out with Brian Short. I could have killed him. . .' His voice tailed off but his hand still clung.

'Brian dropped off a note from Karen that Saturday morning!'

'It was none of my business anyway!' he muttered. 'I kept telling myself that, but I still had to lash out, to hurt you because I was hurting so much myself, wanting you so badly and not knowing what to do about it.'

'So where do we go from here?' she asked him, wanting to hear the words of love that would seal his commitment to her and set her own love free.

'Help me sit up,' he said, dropping her hand as he struggled to raise his body against the pillows, despite the heavy cast that pinned him to the bed. She pressed the button to raise the bed-head, and reached out to help him, but he caught her in his arms and held her close.

'I've got to do it right,' he told her with great seriousness, 'because, wherever he is, old Josh will be watching.'

He lifted one hand to doff an imaginary hat, and made a cramped little bow as he said, 'Jo Armitage, my darling doctor, will you accept this gift of passion-ate, all-embracing love I place so humbly at your feet, and do me the great honour of becoming my wife?'

She felt his eyes burning steadily into hers, and knew, despite the mocking laughter in the words, that he was deadly serious. The depth of his feeling for her and the anxiety that haunted him as he waited for her reply showed in the whitening strain of his already pale face and the slight trembling of the fingers that had regathered her hand.

'I think Rosie has already answered for me,' she told him, leaning over him to press her hot, thirsting lips against his cold ones, as her body throbbed its own response, enchantment bubbling in her veins and a spangle of bright starfire bursting behind her closed eyelids.

SUMMER SPECIAL!

Four exciting new Romances for the price of three

Each Romance features British heroines and their encounters with dark and desirable Mediterranean men. *Plus, a free Elmlea recipe booklet inside every pack.*

So sit back and enjoy your sumptuous summer reading pack and indulge yourself with the free Elmlea recipe ideas.

Available July 1994   Price £5.70

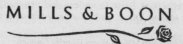

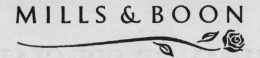

MILLS & BOON

LOVE ON CALL

The books for enjoyment this month are:

TROUBLED HEARTS Christine Adams
SUNLIGHT AND SHADOW Frances Crowne
PARTNERS IN PRIDE Drusilla Douglas
A TESTING TIME Meredith Webber

♥ ♥ ♥ ♥ ♥

Treats in store!

Watch next month for the following absorbing stories:

HEARTS OUT OF TIME Judith Ansell
THE DOCTOR'S DAUGHTER Margaret Barker
MIDNIGHT SUN Rebecca Lang
ONE CARING HEART Marion Lennox

LOVE ON CALL
4 FREE BOOKS AND 2 FREE GIFTS
FROM MILLS & BOON

Capture all the drama and emotion of a hectic medical world when you accept 4 Love on Call romances PLUS a cuddly teddy bear and a mystery gift - absolutely FREE and without obligation. And, if you choose, go on to enjoy 4 exciting Love on Call romances every month for only £1.80 each! Be sure to return the coupon below today to: Mills & Boon Reader Service, FREEPOST, PO Box 236, Croydon, Surrey CR9 9EL.

✂ — — — — — — [**NO STAMP REQUIRED**] — — — — — —

YES! Please rush me 4 FREE Love on Call books and 2 FREE gifts! Please also reserve me a Reader Service subscription, which means I can look forward to receiving 4 brand new Love on Call books for only £7.20 every month, postage and packing FREE. If I choose not to subscribe, I shall write to you within 10 days and still keep my FREE books and gifts. I may cancel or suspend my subscription at any time. I am over 18 years. Please write in BLOCK CAPITALS.

Ms/Mrs/Miss/Mr _____ **EP63D**

Address _____

_____

Postcode _____ Signature _____

Offer closes 30th September 1994. The right is reserved to refuse an application and change the terms of this offer. One application per household. Offer not valid to current Love on Call subscribers. Offer valid only in UK and Eire. Overseas readers please write for details. Southern Africa write to IBS, Private Bag, X3010, Randburg, 2125, South Africa. You may be mailed with offers from other reputable companies as a result of this application. Please tick box if you would prefer not to receive such offers ☐